THE PHAR MA CIST

BIOGRAPHY

JUSTIN DAVID is a writer and photographer. A child of Wolverhampton, he has lived and worked in East London for most of his adult life. He graduated from the MA Creative and Life Writing at Goldsmiths, University of London, has read at *Polari* at Royal Festival Hall, and is a founder member of *Leather Lane Writers*. His writing has appeared in many print and online anthologies and his debut novella was published by *Salt* as part of their Modern Dreams series.

His photography collection of nocturnal performers, *Night Work*, has been exhibited in London at venues including Jackson's Lane. His photographic works have appeared on the pages of numerous magazines including: *Attitude, Beige, Classical Music Magazine, Fluid, Gay Times, Gaze, GlitterWolf, Muso, Out There, Pink Paper, Polari Magazine, QX* and *Time Out*.

Justin is one half of *Inkandescent*—a new publishing venture with his partner, Nathan Evans. Their first offering, *Threads*, featuring Nathan's poetry and Justin's photography, was long-listed for the Polari First Book Prize. It was supported using public funding by Arts Council England and is available in paperback and ebook.

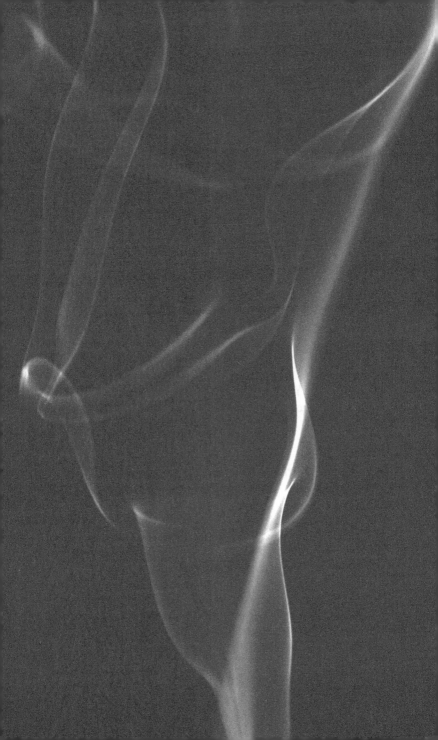

THE PHAR MA C|ST

Justin David

INKANDESCENT

Published by Inkandescent, 2020

Publisher's note: a version of *The Pharmacist* was published
by Salt Publishing in 2014. Another version was included in
He's Done Ever So Well for Himself by Justin David,
published by Inkandescent in 2018

A CIP catalogue record for this book
is available from the British Library

Printed in the UK by Clays Ltd, Elcograf S.p.A.

ISBN 978-1-912620-04-3 (paperback)
ISBN 978-1-912620-05-0 (Kindle ebook)

1 3 5 7 9 10 8 6 4 2
www.inkandescent.co.uk

For Nathan Evans

'Our hearts are connected by a string,
as slender and as silken and strong
as that which a spider spins.'

'We don't see things as they are,
We see things as we are.'
– ANAIS NIN

'To paint oneself is to paint the portrait of a man
who is going to die. Relationships are mirrors.
The painter looks to the mirror to paint himself,
The lover looks into his lover to love himself.'
– ROBERT O. LENKIEWICZ

Billy is in his usual spot, leaning against the wall of the pub, taking photographs and savouring a beer after a stressful week at work. Through half-closed eyes, he zooms in on an old man talking with the flower seller on the opposite side of Columbia Road flower market. A bunch of bright pink gerberas is being wrapped up, and then money is exchanging hands. Even from where he's standing, Billy can see it's more money than the cost of a bunch of flowers and the flower seller is counting it out to the old man, not the other way round. Billy lowers the camera. The old man in the cream linen suit turns and for a split second, in the fiery glare of summer, across the street, he and Billy are smiling at each other. Billy acknowledges him with a nod. But then, he appears a little self-conscious under his cream Panama. The old man looks back, shiftily, at the flower seller who's nudging him with the bunch of gerberas. He takes the flowers. Billy watches them nodding agreeably to each other and, as they are shaking hands, he sees the old man quickly pass something, a tiny packet, to the flower seller who winks as they exchange inaudible words.

Often, on Sunday lunchtimes, Billy comes here to take photographs and chat to the traders selling the last of their flowers. He's attracted by the atmosphere of the market and enjoys the eccentric postmodern revivalists, in their vintage costumes and designer accessories, who posture and parade as if the street were a catwalk. Yet on this occasion, he's gripped by this debonair gentleman. Billy disregards the transaction he thought might have taken place. It's the old man he's interested in. He must

13

live locally. Billy's seen him at least three times before, here on the street. Unmistakable. When the old man walks, trailing rich aromatic smoke from his pipe, he holds himself taut and regal. This graceful image of a man is enough to spark Billy's interest for unconventional behaviour, and he manages a couple of good shots of the man, amid his photographs of the flowers.

From his place in the sunlight, he observes the old man doff his hat and say 'goodbye' to the flower seller, punctuated by a flourish of his hand.

Look at that, thinks Billy, the flair, the twirl. He loves that the man doesn't conform to any normal code of behaviour. Swanning swiftly through the crowds of fashionably dressed people carrying freshly cut flowers, the old gentleman disappears round the corner into Laburnum Road. Billy follows quickly to see if he can get another shot to take back to the studio. The old man fascinates him and he wonders if he may have found a new subject. The gentleman heads down the East End street towards the Victorian maisonettes where Billy lives. It's a great surprise to him to see the old man take a key from his pocket and slip into the communal entrance of his building; Billy's building. 'Oh my God!' Billy says out loud, before reaching the front door. 'He lives upstairs.'

After that, Billy doesn't see his mystery man again for days. While he's curious about the old man living upstairs, he's hardly had time to unpack, let alone introduce himself to the neighbours. Perhaps even a week goes by before he hears anything more than the old man's footsteps, or the cackle of friends sloshing wine around upstairs. One morning, they meet in the little entrance hall to their maisonettes. They greet each other with the stiff, ceremonious air of businessmen, neither quite knowing how to react, having already met but not met.

'Albert Power,' offers the old man, replacing the pipe in his mouth, freeing up his remaining hand.

'Billy Monroe,' he returns. They shake hands, but with Billy beaming right at him, Albert's eyes fall uncomfortably to the floor. He's carrying a brown leather carry case. 'Working?' Billy asks, nodding to the case.

'Er, no,' Albert says and moves the case guardedly behind his legs. 'I don't work.' Billy wonders what might be inside and why a retired old gentleman would be carrying such a thing.

Albert steps towards the interior door of his flat, adjacent to Billy's door. 'Well, neighbours we are,' he says, inserting his key into the lock.

Billy allows his voice to deepen. 'I've knocked a couple of times since I moved in, but I keep missing you.'

'Not to worry,' Albert replies, hurriedly. 'We must keep different hours. Ships in the night and all that.' He lets himself in and turns back to Billy, now that the ice has been broken, correcting what appears as plain aloofness. A streak of sunlight through the street door catches one side of Albert's face. 'But you're here *now*. *You're* not at work *today*?' Albert asks, one eyeball gleaming like a pebble of tiger's eye.

There is a charged moment when their eyes meet, in which Billy feels a knowledge pass between them. It's the kind of cruisy look he only usually gets from young guys in bars and clubs. Billy knows he should look away, but Albert doesn't, so *he* doesn't. He feels something there—the weird sensation, perhaps, that they knew each other before. 'I'm on holiday from work,' Billy replies, and breaks his gaze.

'Ah.' Albert nods. 'You live alone?'

Billy has no reason to be anything other than transparent now, but he finds himself saying, 'Yes. I live alone.'

'No… girlfriend?'

'No.' Not a lie. Though in omitting the fact that he's actually in a relationship, he knows he's not being honest either.

'Oh?'

'What?'

'It's just that I thought I'd seen someone else coming and going.'

Billy looks up and smiles at Albert's blatant prying. 'That's Jamie. He's been helping, since I moved in,' Billy says, still being opaque. That puts an end to it, for now at least, allowing a silent moment in which Billy takes in every physical detail. Good muscles and bone structure give Albert a taut appearance. He looks younger than his attire would suggest and Billy thinks he would look more at home on the set of a Tennessee Williams play. He's curious to see an off-white shirt, collars fraying at the sides of his neck.

'Well, at last we meet,' Albert says. 'Pop up for a drink some-time.' Albert's gaze falls, less discreetly this time, over the length of Billy's body, as if stroking each downy hair on Billy's skin with his eyes. 'I'm in and out. Just knock.' Albert turns to enter his flat.

'Thanks. I will,' Billy says. He smiles and walks out into the sunlit street.

§

'I prefer Dalston to Kentish Town. And that estate agent was a right slimy fucker.'

Billy glances sideways at Jamie. It's the liveliest he's seen him for a long time. Real joy. The end of Billy's cigarette burns to the filter and he flicks it into the gutter. There are two pubs on this street. The first one they come to has a beer garden. 'Shall we stop here for a pint and talk?'

'Sure,' Jamie says.

When Billy walks over to Jamie with two pints of lager, the sales materials are already spread out on the table. Jamie looks up, takes his beer. 'Lovely' he says, and he nods as Billy slides onto the bench. 'You okay?'

Billy has hit a wall. The painting isn't happening. The existing ones aren't really selling. He's going through the motions while Jamie's doing so well. And it shows. Jamie is now splashing out on boutique clothes. 'We need a fresh start. We need something new,' Billy says.

'Well, looking at these… loft apartment in Shoreditch, warehouse work-live unit in Clapton… I'm not sure we can really afford any of them, especially after all those fancy holidays we've been having.'

17

'We can't live like this all our lives, constantly at the mercy of a greedy landlord.' Billy rubs his hands over his jeans, thighs torn and threadbare and not in an ironic way. They'd agonised over the idea of moving in together ever since Jamie had returned from New Mexico, and that had been ages ago. Despite Jamie being established in his new job at the Walter's Gallery and being rather more solvent than he'd ever been in his life, Billy actually found he enjoyed living alone. It has taken him until now to relinquish his freedom.

'I'm fed up of living out of a suitcase. It's time to set down some roots.'

He looks at Jamie studying him, working him out. 'We don't have to do this now, Billy. You know, financially, it might be better if we wait.'

Billy fiddles with his fag packet. 'I don't want to wait. Let's take a risk.'

Jamie holds one of the sheets of paper up. 'Dalston?'

'Dalston.' Billy feels his stomach drop. In his mind, there is the echo of a life now given up. He necks his beer.

'You're drinking fast?'

Billy shrugs. 'Nothing else to do. You going to book another appointment, then?'

'Leave it all to me.'

§

Another summer day, Billy is sitting on the wall outside the flats, like a lonely teenager in the school holidays. He's smoking a spliff, wistfully reading a paperback. Albert is quickly becoming one of his obsessions. He's started to note the times Albert leaves and returns to the flat, or what he wears; sometimes the cream linen suit, sometimes a shirt without a jacket, but always the Panama.

For a moment, a movement of cool air across his bare arms causes him to slip out of his fictional dream. He lets the book rest on his leg and turns to look up at Albert's open window. The gentle breeze catches the lacy curtain making it billow playfully, before Billy returns to his book. Then he's pleasantly startled by a voice behind him. 'Good day, Billy.' Albert's leaning out of his first-floor window, doffing his hat. 'Isn't the light beautiful?'

'Alright, Albert.' Billy smiles over his shoulder.

'Been stood up?' Albert asks.

'You could say that. I was waiting for…' He stops himself again before saying Jamie's name, '…my friend.' Why is he holding back? He knows the old man finds him desirable. He's enjoying being a tease, waiting to see where this will lead.

Albert winks. 'If you're at a loose end, come up. I'll open a bottle of wine.'

§

At last, together in the same space, Billy drinks red wine with his new friend. It's as if they have always known each other. In this short space of time, he's learned that Albert's favourite authors are Genet and Proust, that he never eats red meat on a Sunday and that he once had dinner with Dusty Springfield.

Billy stands in the open bay window where Albert had stood earlier. He wonders where Jamie could have got to. Maybe he'd had to work after all. This is happening more frequently since he started that blasted job at the Walter's Gallery. He's so good at his job, they just want more and more of him. The thought lingers at the back of his throat like a bit of dry bread until he washes it down with a zealous gulp of red wine.

Cradling the glass, he leans out into the sunshine, intermittently eyeing up a neighbour washing his car. The street is ablaze with gold and green—dappled sunlight pushing through the gaps in the foliage of the sycamores lining the street. Albert stands, holding the bottle of red wine. 'Vada the bona dish on the omi-palone!' he says, extending every vowel sound, curling his words like ornate calligraphy. He's come to stand next to Billy, to stare down at the neighbour. The palm of Albert's hand gently rests on his back, warmth spreading through the fabric of his vest. Billy turns and presses his arse against the windowsill. 'Eh?'

Albert pours more wine into Billy's almost empty glass. 'I said, look at the rear end on that gorgeous queen.' Albert puts the bottle down and gulps his wine.

It takes Billy a moment to register. 'Ah, Polari. I haven't heard that for ages,' he says, but still feels a little bewildered. 'Who?'

'That guy next door.' Albert nods his head towards the man in the street. 'Don't pretend. I saw you. Couldn't take your eyes off him.'

Billy looks over his shoulder at the man who has dropped his sponge and now has his mobile phone clamped to the side of his face. He's sneering and flaring his nostrils, looking busy. He takes lots of very quick, small steps, down the tree-lined street, shoulders pivoting forwards and backwards. After having been misled by an image of butch masculinity, this little display makes them both giggle. Billy turns back to see Albert smiling to himself, walking across the room to throw his hat on a coat stand. 'Dolly capello, old fruit,' Billy says, complimenting Albert on his hat. They both suddenly crack into laughter, surprised but united now, across the generation gap, by the ancient gentleman's slang.

For a moment there's a silence in which they stand looking at each other. 'So, what do you do?' Albert finally says.

The question makes Billy squirm. He ponders a second before announcing, 'I'm an artist.' He knows if he's ever going to live the life he wants he must get used to defining himself so. It seems such an airy-fairy thing to say—not really a proper job.

'I knew you had to be a painter. First time I met you, in the hall, I smelt the turps. Though, I suppose when I saw you loitering in the flower market, from the way you were dressed, I thought you might have owned one of those trendy art galleries on Columbia Road.'

'You saw me?' Billy acts surprised, but of course he knows that Albert had seen him that day. He covers a smile with his hand.

'Oh come off it. You were watching me!' Albert teases. 'You even nodded at me.' His eyes glint and his cheeks flush pink perhaps with the wine. 'But didn't you say you were on *holiday*, the other day?'

Billy explains that he works part-time for an arts trust.

'Must be difficult,' Albert says. 'Working in an office as well as fitting in your creative activities.'

He's relaxed, even though the old man continues to fire question after question at him. There seems nothing guarded about Albert. From the outside, who would guess they only just met?

Billy looks around the room. It's a large space with bare floorboards and a thick rag rug in the middle. Floor-to-ceiling bookshelves run along the left-hand side of the bay window. In front of the window there's a tatty cream chaise longue, and in the corner, to the right, a writing bureau, on top of which sits an emerald green glass vase, containing eight bright pink gerberas. Billy counts each stalk and wonders if Albert has always chosen that colour.

'I'm easing myself into the painting again,' Billy says. 'But no doubt just as I build enough momentum to work towards the next show, I'll run out of money and be back to the grind.'

'Got to stay positive, Billy. You'll make it work.'

Billy continues to gaze around the room. In front of the bookshelves, there is a well-worn ox-blood leather Chesterfield and a standard lamp with a dusty cream shade. On a glass-topped coffee table sit a few books and a scattering of magazines. Some of them are pornographic, which strikes Billy as rather unusual. Is Albert too lazy to clear up, or is he making a statement?

'But you'll continue to paint?'

Billy nods. 'Right! That's enough,' he says, flopping down onto the Chesterfield, halting further interrogation. 'You've been quizzing me ever since I arrived. What about you?'

'Me? I'm an open book. Not all that interesting, mind.' Albert bites his bottom lip as if to feign shyness. 'I am all your failed expectations in a man,' he says sadly. Billy lifts the bottle of wine and Albert pushes his glass towards him. He pours two more glasses and Albert swallows almost half of his in one gulp.

'Well, you must have a pretty pension to keep this place on. What did you do? I mean work-wise—for a living?'

'Life doesn't cost a lot now. There's no mortgage on this place. But there are no savings and no pension either, only what I get from the state and that's next to nothing. I've done some acting. Used to be a singer. All a blur now. I managed a very nice restaurant in Soho, once. But mainly, I just got by.'

'Just got by?' Billy questions. 'I can hear the jangle of old money in your voice.'

'Darling Boy!' Albert says, pointing his finger. 'You must not make assumptions about people based on the way they speak.'

'I had you down as an aristocrat. Blue blood.'

'We're not all high fliers, Billy. I'm just a survivor.'

'Well at least you have your home. How *are* you surviving?'

Albert pauses in contemplation. Billy doesn't know much about him, but he senses Albert is about to open up. 'Billy, I hardly know you. But I feel we have a connection.'

23

'Me too.' Billy gives him a sexy little smile, confirming a mutual trust.

'Okay, well if you can keep a secret…'

'I thought you were an open book?' Billy sits forward keenly.

'Everyone has things that they keep to themselves.' Albert slumps next to Billy on the Chesterfield and starts to talk, slurring his words a little. 'I think it's really important, at whatever cost, to be true to oneself. I hate spending my time in drag for other people's convenience.' Albert sloshes back more wine. 'I mean *drag* in terms of putting on a performance. You know, like wearing a mask, covering up the self.

'This is the way I see it. Most folks want to get married and have babies. So they have a baby, and they do everything they can to mould it, shape it, and dress it into what they think it should be. And they set this child on a path towards where they think it should be going.

'You know, one is lucky if you grow up feeling comfortable being that person, being that shape, being on that path. And you can forget to think for yourself. One can get so far down that path with the job and the wife and the car, that before you know it, the whole process starts again, of making more babies to mould and shape, mould and shape… and oh…' He pauses and swallows, then continues almost without drawing breath. 'But for some of us, no matter how hard we try, we just don't fit a particular shape. And we start thinking for ourselves. And we come to a fork in the road. And you just know you've got to make this choice, because when you're different, if you wear those

24

clothes and stay on that path, when you know you really should be somewhere else, then you're just doing drag. Do you see what I'm talking about Billy?'

Billy is completely absorbed. 'I think so. Yeah. But I don't really understand what this has to do with money?'

'Well, when you make that choice, when you take that fork in the road, you might have to turn around to your folks and say, 'Yes, thanks for that. But no.' With that, you're on your own. Surviving means you might end up doing things you had never expected.'

Billy waits for a moment, expecting a punch line. 'So come on then. What's your secret?'

Albert turns to Billy and looks directly at him. 'I'm in pharmaceuticals.'

Billy narrows his eyes at Albert.

'You ever go dancing?'

'God—all the time,' Billy says.

'You know The Palais? On Kingsland Road?'

'Yeah. Been there lots of times. There's a fantastic Trance night on Fridays.'

Albert's eyes widen. 'You've never seen me there?'

'You?'

'Yes, *me*, strangely enough! Old man in a Panama. Impossible to miss.'

'No.'

'I deal drugs in there.'

Billy feels his chin drop. 'You're kidding?'

'Close your mouth, Billy. You look like you're trying to catch flies.' Albert swallows more wine.

'I don't understand.'

'It's not hard, Billy. Every Friday night I go to The Palais and I sell drugs to the clubbers.'

'What kind of drugs?'

'What kind of drugs do you think? Coke, speed, pills. A little bit of acid sometimes, but mainly E's.'

'Albert… you're an old man,' Billy says.

'Thank you for pointing that out.'

Billy rolls around, uncoiling in his place on the Chesterfield. 'Well, of course—a very *well-preserved* old man,' he giggles.

Albert smiles, his eyes sparkling, full of danger.

Billy sits quietly staring at him, pondering the old man for several minutes. Albert smiles back without complaint, until Billy asks, 'What are E's like?'

'You mean you've never done one?' Albert runs his fingers through silver hair.

'Never done anything, except a bit of grass.' Billy looks at the clock on Albert's bureau. They have been chatting for hours. An empty bottle of wine stands on the coffee table and a second, half empty, is in Albert's hand refilling Billy's glass. The sunlight is changing. It's lower now and passes through the window, causing Billy's wine glass to sparkle like a giant ruby.

'I thought you said you'd been to The Palais on a Friday night?'

'I have, but I've never done an E.'

'You? A man in his twenties, dancing around half-naked in

The Palais, never done an E?'

Billy laughs. 'Well, I suppose, in the past, my attention was mainly on my work. The students who did drugs at art college didn't get first class degrees. It would have been no good, me doing drugs. I can't even open a box of chocolates without finishing the lot.'

'Ha. I see. But most people who hang out on the club scene, especially those of your age, have tried it at least once. Part of the territory.'

Billy shrugs. 'Never been offered.'

'Never lived.' Albert chuckles and strokes Billy's head.

Billy is alert like a boy on his first day of school. 'Tell me what it's like,' he says, lightening the tone of his voice, playing innocent. He kicks off his trainers, falls back onto the sofa and breathes in sun-warmed leather.

'Hard to say. Like nothing you've ever felt in your life. Like being in a dream state.' Albert flutters his hands in the air, pretending to scatter fairy dust. When his hand drops, it falls casually onto Billy's shoulder. Billy allows it to rest there.

'Can't you be more specific? Dream state? Call yourself a drug dealer?'

'I'm an expert on all drugs,' Albert says. He undoes the top buttons of his shirt and removes his cravat. For a man of his age, Billy notes, his skin is in very good condition—only a slight sagginess where one might expect to see a more developed dewlap. His strong jawline reminds Billy of Marlon Brando. 'I've never ingested any substance without first knowing about all the highs

27

and the side effects. But with E, the experience is slightly different for everyone. Generally, with ecstasy, it's all about empathy. If people around you are enjoying themselves, chances are, you'll pick up on that vibe.'

'They make you feel horny, don't they?' Billy asks, still playing dumb.

'Yes. There's that too.' Albert smiles.

A July breeze of warm air moves through the open window. Sounds float in from the street—birdsong, traffic, the wind through the trees.

'What else? People die, don't they?'

'There are risks, I suppose, but really, the few deaths that have occurred have been the result of carelessness. Overheating, or else over-hydration and all that stuff.'

'You trying to sell to me?'

'Darling Boy, I'm not a drug *pusher*. I sell to those who *use* them. If you want to try one, you are more than welcome.'

Billy is surprised by this suggestion. A man of his age, sitting around popping Es, seemed unconventional to say the least. 'Don't you worry about stuff?'

'Like what?' Albert says, clearing his throat.

'Short-term memory loss. Alzheimer's. You read things, don't you?'

'When you reach my state of decrepitude, you stop worrying. Look at me, I'm seventy. Nothing wrong with my memory. And, Darling Boy, for every brain cell that has died, a new door has opened to a magical world.'

There's a wry twinkle in Albert's eye. 'People who do drugs always say stuff like that,' Billy says, deliberately juvenile.

'I've explored corners of my mind which would've been otherwise unreachable. It has helped me to recall events from my childhood with incredible clarity.'

'What about the hard stuff? Done that?'

'I've done everything,' Albert says.

Billy rubs the insides of his legs in anticipation. 'Everything?'

'We live in a chemical world, Billy Monroe. Everyone needs some kind of medicine.' Billy forgives him the use of his surname. It makes him feel like a pupil being addressed by a teacher but he knows that Albert is playing his game.

'What for?' Billy asks.

'When I'm tired, I snort a little speed. When I'm restless, I have a bit of pot. And if I'm feeling stuck. I mean, if I feel troubled by something, I'll smoke a bit of opium to help me get through it. If I can't sleep, I slip a little something in my tea.'

'Speed? When you're tired?'

Albert shrugs. 'From time to time. Gets the vacuuming done.'

'Albert Power!' There, switching roles—he's equal now. 'You must have a liver like a piece of leather.' He sits forward, trembling.

Albert stands, moves to the writing bureau, pulls open the front and lifts out a tiny bag of white tablets, shaking out a handful before disappearing through a beaded curtain into the kitchen. A moment later, he returns with two pint glasses of water and sits down next to Billy. Albert places his hand over

29

the table and lets the tablets fall onto the glass surface. For a moment, Billy looks at them. Then he leans and picks one up, rolls it between his thumb and forefinger and examines its tiny logo.

'Mitsubishi. Bona doobs!'

'Eh?' Billy misses the slang again.

'Don't you know your Polari, Darling Boy? Doobs. Drugs. These are good ones. Pure MDMA. Lovely trip.'

Billy's mobile phone buzzes in his pocket. He pulls it out to read the text message. It's from Jamie.

> *Really sorry, Billy. Had to work late.*
> *I'm not going to make it.*

Billy frowns and stuffs the phone back in his jeans.

'Problem?' Albert asks.

'Not at all.' He smiles coyly, puts the pill to his mouth, lets it touch his tongue. 'It tastes bitter,' he says, pulling a face.

'Swallow it.'

The glass of water trembles in Billy's hands. Albert swallows his pill and smiles. 'See? Not dead yet.'

After washing it down with water, Billy leans back and puts his feet up on Albert's coffee table, waiting for something to happen. Albert's right. Billy is surprised, even by himself, that he has reached his mid-twenties and still hasn't tried this. It makes him feel young and naïve. They sit quietly for a minute. 'What now?' Billy asks.

'Be patient. All will be revealed.' Albert stands up abruptly. 'Music!' he says, and moves around the coffee table with the grace of a ballet dancer, slipping his hand beneath the glass and sliding open a drawer. It takes him a moment to select a disc.

Restlessly, Billy gets up and walks to the window behind the chaise longue and looks out onto the street. The shadows along the road are longer now as the sun moves even lower. But it's still very bright. 'I love these long, hot summer evenings,' he says, stretching his arms above his head. He lets his eyes follow his hands as the psychedelic folk of Goldfrapp's *Felt Mountain* begins to play. Billy breathes out. 'I love this,' he says.

'Seminal album,' Albert says.

The silver bracelet on Billy's wrist catches the sunlight. When he lets his eyes fall again, they are caught by the refracted light from a collection of coloured glass vessels on the windowsill—red, yellow, green and blue glass, tall and thin, short and wide, straight and curved. Billy marvels at the new colours created where light passes through more than one layer of glass, one in front of the other; red and yellow making amber, blue and red making amethyst.

'The warm air is lovely, isn't it?' Albert finally says, in agreement. 'So you like the sun?'

'I'm a real baby. Hate winter. Going to work in the dark and all that. Summer is my favourite time of year.' He continues to look down onto the tree-lined street, knowing Albert's eyes are lingering on him, sketching, tracing the curve of his bicep, moving across his groin. Then, to tease the old man,

31

he deliberately turns back to face the room. Albert is taken by surprise, and spins to face the CD player, face reddening. Billy looks away to spare him embarrassment but can't help smiling. 'I can't feel anything at all.'

'Good God, child! You only swallowed it a few minutes ago. Give it chance.'

Albert's electronic sounds perforate the air beautifully. He returns to the sofa and pats the seat next to him. 'Come on, Darling Boy, it will come when it's ready.' He picks up Billy's book, which has been lying face down on the coffee table next to Billy's digital camera. 'Is that what you were reading, out there on the wall?'

'Look how splendid the light is in this room.' Billy points to the glass ornaments. 'Have you seen how the colour from that wine glass is being projected onto the wall?'

Albert turns the book over and moves it up closer to his eyes. 'Ah, *Catcher in the Rye*,' he says.

Billy tilts his head to face the ceiling, gazes at the room, spangled with coloured light. 'Look, Albert.'

'Yes, Darling Boy.' Albert nods, drops the book back on the coffee table and pulls his nose up.

'Why the face?'

'It's the kind of book one discovers when one is sixteen.'

'Listen to you!' Billy says.

'Well, you are an artist after all. I'd've thought you'd have read all those angst-ridden books by now. How old *are* you?' Albert asks.

Billy goes to answer and then stops himself. 'How old do I look?'

'Ha. You're asking for trouble now!'

Billy throws his head back proudly and smoothes down his eyebrows. 'I'm twenty-four.'

Albert pouts. 'I'd have guessed at thirty.'

'Cheeky sod.' Billy punches Albert playfully on the shoulder.

'Though for your manner, mind,' Albert says, 'and your confidence. But you do have the complexion of a youth.'

Billy closes his eyes and takes a deep breath. The fresh air seems to flush through his whole body, refreshing all the way to the tips of his feet. When he opens his eyes again, he says, 'I don't think anything is going to happen.'

'Well, I suppose you might be a bit disappointed. Who knows? Just wait. It's better if you don't think about it. Listen to the music.'

Billy sits forward and thumbs through the pornography on the coffee table—groups of naked men in leather harnesses, tattoos, piercings, just his sort of thing. Then he lets his hands explore a plain-covered, glossy coffee-table book—*The Complete Guide to Recreational Psychoactives*. As he turns the pages, the silver bands on his fingers sparkle in the half-light. He reads out loud the descriptions of random substances. 'Heroin… a potent painkiller derived from morphine… produces an overwhelming sense of well-being, elation and blissful apathy… notoriously addictive, it can lead to complex physical withdrawal.' He continues to let the pages of the book fall open at random.

'Gamma-hydroxybutyrate or GHB is a sedative drug which, used in the right quantities, induces an experience of disequilibria, a euphoric state in which the user has an increased capacity for tactile sensitivity...' He looks up at Albert. 'I can't believe there's actually a book on all this stuff.'

Albert shrugs. 'A drug user's Bible.'

'You can say that again.' Billy sits back for a while, in silence. He strokes the blonde hairs on his forearms while the music tips into something more electronic. Albert sips water, stretches, postures in an exaggerated theatrical gesture and slumps back into the Chesterfield. He breathes in deeply, filling his lungs before relaxing next to Billy, who shifts uneasily in his seat.

'Getting fidgety, Darling Boy?'

'Yeah.' Billy begins to play with the zip on a cushion.

Albert flicks him playfully on the shoulder. 'See! It's beginning to work—a touch of adrenaline. That's the edginess you can feel.'

Billy rubs his sweaty palms on his jeans and looks at Albert.

'Look at your eyes!' Albert says.

'What's wrong with them?'

'Pupils are dilated, eyes are all sparkly. You look very beautiful.'

Billy watches Albert smiling warmly at him. Then he lets his eyes fall shut. Ever changing kaleidoscopic patterns spiral behind his eyelids. His palms tingle.

'Do you feel like you're glowing?' Albert asks.

'Yeah, and light as a feather.' Billy moves to the edge of his seat and lets his head fall into his hands, moving gently, synchronised with the music. 'Butterflies in my stomach. I think I can feel it,

Albert. I think it's beginning to work.'

'I know, Darling Boy. I can feel it too.'

Billy tries to grasp the feeling in his head but it is indefinable. Maybe like a pillowcase of feathers exploding in his head. So soft and subtle, but intense and powerful all at once. 'Oh God. Albert, can you feel this?'

Albert doesn't answer. Moments later Billy lifts his head out of his hands and opens his eyes. He sees Albert swallowing another pill, washing it down with water.

'What are you doing?' Billy asks.

'Oh, stop frowning. It takes a bit more for me these days. People develop a tolerance.'

Billy wonders if it will rot his brain away. He notices Albert catch the look on his face. 'I don't do this *every* weekend,' Albert says, defensively.

'Not in The Palais on Fridays?' Billy imagines him stalking around in the darkness, snaking his way through a dance floor of clubbers, or rocking from side to side in a corner somewhere.

'That wouldn't be good for business. No.'

Billy feels suddenly disappointed. It's gone. The feeling has just gone away. He sits back wondering if he's imagined it and waits to see if it returns.

'I remember my first pill vividly. It's not something you ever forget.'

'Oh my God.' Billy interrupts and collapses into his own hands. He can feel the drug beginning to work again. 'Can you feel this? Tell me you can feel this.' He sighs deeply and then sits back on the sofa with his eyes shut.

Albert lifts his palms in a sign of indifference.

'This is blowing my mind.' Billy holds his arms out in front of him. Tiny beads of sweat have begun to appear on the surface of his skin, trickling along the lines of his tattoos. He touches the clammy skin at the nape of his neck.

'What can you feel?' Albert asks playfully.

'It's... indescribable. The best mood I've ever been in.' All the anxiety he's been carrying around seems to be falling away. He thinks about Jamie not turning up. Earlier, he'd been concerned, but now it's okay. It doesn't matter; all is well in his world.

'Bliss,' Albert says.

'Perfect.' Billy opens his eyes. 'Can we change the music?'

'Do whatever you like.'

Billy moves around the coffee table to view Albert's collection of CDs. His evening with Albert has been very easy. Without the history normal friendships require, he feels they both trust each other unreservedly. Billy fingers the tiny bag of pills on the table. 'Who would have thought that something so tiny could cause such an effect? Albert, I feel... how do you explain this—so many feelings all at once? There aren't words for it. I feel drunk. No, not drunk. It's not like alcohol, but I feel... Oh God, it's coming again...'

Billy, on his knees now, sinks forward and leans over the coffee table, head-in-hands as another cloud of feather-down explodes in his head and causes another torrent of pleasure to rain over his entire body.

'You alright, Billy? It's coming on a bit strong for you, isn't it?'

Billy runs his hands over his hair, feeling how wonderful it is to touch his own head, his own flesh. Then he moves and flicks through the CD collection. It's a jumble: Mozart next to Kraftwerk, David Bowie next to Sarah Vaughan. '*Six* different versions of La Wally?' Billy remarks.

'Yes. But Callas is the best.' Albert marks the air with a finger.

A few moments later, the drug has taken full grip over Billy. He can't be arsed to change the music. He sinks into the Chesterfield next to Albert, swaying and breathing deeply. He moans softly as the waves of blissful pleasure move through his body.

Albert rolls a joint. Billy is mesmerised by the intricate process, which Albert goes through, first sprinkling the tobacco and then the grass into the Rizla paper. Watching Albert deftly rolling it between thumb and index fingers, until it becomes a perfectly formed spliff, makes him feel even more bizarrely relaxed. He can feel himself going cross-eyed. Billy looks again at the clock. This time he can't see the hands anymore. But he knows it's much later. The light is beginning to fade.

He closes his eyes, gently pulls the bottom of his vest up a little to feel the soft ladder of hair above his navel. He sighs deeply. 'I feel like I'm in touch with the universe. In touch with God,' he goes on. 'Everything suddenly makes sense. Or maybe it doesn't. But everything just feels right... safe.'

He lets out a deep, refreshing breath again and shifts in his seat. 'I love you, Albert,' he says without even thinking about it.

For a moment, he wonders why he would say such a thing. But it feels perfectly natural. He does love Albert.

Albert gives a little laugh. 'I love you too, Darling Boy,' he says with exaggerated warmth. He ruffles Billy's short crop again, lights the joint and takes a long drag. Billy, greedily, takes the joint from his fingers and starts to smoke it himself.

'Look at the state you're in. That'll knock you for six.'

'In for a penny, in for a pound.' Billy inhales long and hard and then hands it back. He closes his eyes and feels himself disappearing into an invisible cloud of delight, moaning and swaying to the music. 'I'm so hot. It's warm in here, isn't it?' He tugs at his vest and peels it away from his body. He examines the tanned skin of his abdominals glistening with dewy sweat. Albert leans towards him slightly, examining the shiny silver ring that pierces his left nipple. 'No stranger to the gym!'

'Fuck, I feel horny,' Billy moans. He closes his eyes again and begins to gently tease his nipples. He shudders at the intense pleasure achieved with each touch of his fingertips.

'This happens often, Billy. People get horny but find themselves incapable of achieving an erection. I see we don't have that problem.' When Billy opens his eyes, Albert is staring at the large bulge in his jeans.

'What?' Billy moans, and lets his eyes roll back in their sockets.

'Oh, don't mind me,' Albert says, sinks into the sofa. 'I'll just sit here.'

'Yeah,' Billy murmurs, letting his head drop back against the Chesterfield. He strokes his chest, lets his hands wander to his groin, slipping a couple of fingers beneath the waist of his jeans. He pulsates and swells beneath the denim. He watches Albert's eager eyes eating him up. Slowly he pushes his jeans down, over his thighs. His erect penis stands up vertical as he rubs it gently in one hand. With the other, he continues to squeeze the tender, alert flesh of his nipple.

He moans. 'I don't believe I'm doing this.'

'Just let go, Darling Boy.' Albert smiles, seemingly unoffended by the unfolding spectacle.

Billy opens his eyelids again, straining to uncross his eyes. He can see two Albert's waving a spliff at him.

After taking another drag on it, he begins to rub himself harder, more rhythmically as he works towards orgasm, waves of ecstasy crashing through his mind and body—his shiny penis gleaming with pre-cum.

'My head's swimming,' Albert says.

Billy watches Albert watching him, overwhelmed, writhing before Albert's eyes. Albert has remained a gentleman through-out the entire episode. Though at this moment, he takes leave of himself. He leans over towards Billy, grasps him in one hand. For Billy, the sensation of having someone else's fingers around him takes him by surprise. He voluntarily drops his arms to his sides in submission. His hips buck, driving a warm jerky surge from his balls. Albert's hand pushes him toward orgasm, pressing the mound of flesh at the base of Billy's cock. Again, Billy bucks, pushing his hips towards Albert's head.

When Albert slides his wet lips down over Billy's penis, he

gasps with pleasure. Eyes open now, Albert's head nods up and down, before Billy crashes back into the feather pillowcases in his head. He can feel every detail of the moment: Albert's bottom lip rubs along the back of the shaft, his tongue on the 'v' of flesh where the foreskin meets the head. Billy can feel Albert taking all of him in, gorging on him, while he writhes powerlessly underneath him, nearing the end.

Afterwards, there is a religious silence. Billy is sated. He casually strokes his cock. He looks at Albert, whose apparent fascination, perhaps even fixation with him, has turned to a look of melancholy as he seems to survey the room and his few material possessions: a collection of compact discs, a writing bureau, a few books and a leather Chesterfield.

And then a new look of admission crosses his face. There is a frank, matter-of-fact tone in his voice. 'Baggage, Darling Boy,' he begins to soliloquise, seemingly aware that Billy has slipped out of his dream state. 'I try not to carry any baggage. Frightened I might lose it, see? If one doesn't own things, one can't lose them.'

The edges of Billy's vision are disappearing as if someone has taken an eraser and rubbed them out. He lets his eyes fall closed and pretends that he's not really listening while the old man continues. 'Can't hold on, but scared of letting go. *He* was everything to me. When I was with him I knew the truth, but now I just make it up as I go along.'

With who? What truth? Billy's thoughts will not stay solid. They float in and out of his mind.

'Walks in the park, photograph albums, boxes full of trinkets, memories of a life I used to have with him. I can see the day that he came in shades of autumn. Somehow my memories all appear in sepia.' Billy tries to follow Albert's thoughts but they jump around. 'Out there, on the street, sitting on the wall, just like you were, reading a book, smoking a spliff. He used to smoke like a chimney. Took his mind in the end. He looked like James Dean. He was reading *East of Eden*. Thank God you weren't reading Steinbeck. I think I would've had a turn, Darling Boy. Of course the street was still gas-lit then, in those days. Showing my age now.'

Billy gazes at Albert, his eyes staring, unfocused. 'You loved him,' he asks—feeling, understanding Albert's loss.

Albert looks surprised. 'You were listening?' The skin around Albert's eyes is darkened and bruised where blood has flushed to the surface. His cheeks appear hollow. His eyes roll back a little as he begins to trip out. 'I lost him,' he says.

Billy struggles to focus. 'But you had your time together. That's what matters.'

Albert is moving across the room now, gently swaying. 'So precious... precious little...' he continues. 'He had golden brown hair, wavy and swept back. At the temples where the hair was shorter, he had tight little curls. I remember his full red lips, like Elizabeth Siddall in those Pre-Raphaelite paintings. He used to wear those v-neck pullovers and a rugby shirt underneath. I always thought he looked like a farm boy. I loved his soft tanned skin. Not unlike you, little more than a boy with dewy eyes and flawless skin.

'We should have made more of the time. It just slipped through our fingers.' Albert gives Billy a box of tissues. 'Clean yourself up, Darling Boy.'

Billy wipes semen from his skin, dabs at where, so quickly, the warm, sticky liquid has turned cold and watery. He licks the residue from around his fingers where liquid has become dry and crystalline.

'Billy Monroe, this is one of those days you'll never ever be able to relive. But it can never be erased. One day when I'm long gone, you'll look over your shoulder, back down the road we've travelled and I'll be there waving back. You're an angel,' he says, as if addressing someone other than Billy in the room. Then looks directly at him, reconnecting. 'It's been one hell of a journey, hasn't it?'

'Epic,' Billy mumbles.

'Fairy tale,' Albert says.

Billy checks himself once more, looks at his watch and stands up. 'I think I need to go downstairs,' he says. He steps closer to Albert and hugs him tightly. Albert's hands caress Billy's torso and he kisses him on the cheek; a kiss neither of them has managed to plant throughout the entire evening. He kisses the skin below Billy's ear and nuzzles the hollow in-between his neck and collarbone.

'Thank you,' Albert says. 'This has been… a pleasure.' Billy can feel him trembling.

Billy stares over Albert's shoulder at a painting. It's been there all the time, on the wall behind the sofa, a large canvas. Billy is surprised that he hadn't noticed it. The frame is gilt, quietly ornate. There is a photo-realistic quality in the image of a man. An astonishing man with a broad masculine jaw-line and just a touch of femininity in his sharp smile. His skin is dark and smooth, the colours of autumn. His face fills the frame, all but for the brim of a Panama hat resting just above his feline eyebrows. Billy studies it.

Albert steps backward to see why Billy is so dumbfounded. He turns, following Billy's eye line. 'Ah, I wondered why you were so quiet.' Albert bends over the coffee table and collects the leftover ecstasy tablets into the plastic bag and presses together the re-sealable zipper.

'It's you!' Billy says, stunned, looking at the painting.

'Yes. Hard to take in, isn't it?' Albert stuffs the bag into the pocket of Billy's jeans. 'For another time,' he says.

Billy rocks unsteadily again. 'Who painted this? It's the most beautiful thing I've ever seen.'

'*He* did. My love. He finished working on that and faded away. I lost him in life's rear-view mirror. I went back for him but he'd gone.' Albert makes perfect sense to Billy. He can hear the pang of sadness in his voice. 'Who'd have thought I would end up like this? Sad old man, dealing in pharmaceuticals.'

Billy says nothing. He thinks it's sad that there is no painting of Albert's companion. He rouses himself and looks about the room. His eyes fall on the coffee table. 'Can I borrow that book?' he asks. When their eyes meet again, Albert is smiling at him.

§

Billy goes back to his own flat carrying Albert's book—*The Complete Guide to Recreational Psychoactives* and places it on his desk. In stark contrast to the summer light that had pervaded Albert's front room earlier, Billy's back room is now dark, cavernous and magical. He often works by candlelight to hide the peeling wood-chip wallpaper and the rising damp making its way through the cracks.

He's brought home something new, something fresh, and something that will help him connect to the source, enough to get him working again. His desk lamp scarcely lights the cluttered back room that he's been using as a workroom for painting, since he gave up his studio at the arts trust. A red light flashes on the answering machine—probably a message from Jamie. Next to the machine are two recent holiday photographs of him and Jamie. Billy glances at them fondly, stroking the glass of one of the frames with a finger. In one image they are in ski-wear and in the other they're in summer vests in San Francisco. The walls are covered with pieces of paper, notes, doodles, photographs, and magazine cuttings, all to inspire his imagination. Books are strewn across the floor and paintings from his previous exhibitions lie stacked up against the walls. Tonight, however, they seem not to be needed. Even with the drug wearing off, there's a feeling of absolute concentration as he starts to work. He gathers his tools and materials, meticulously laying them out, as a surgeon does before an operation. He stretches a canvas over a frame, mixes paint and prepares the surface of the linen. When he's ready, he begins to paint. The image of a man, head and shoulders, emerges very quickly on the canvas. No preliminary sketches or background materials are gathered. There is no model. The likeness built up, as if projected directly from his own mind. Layer over layer, he builds up the paint, gradually, until the image is formed, like flesh stretching over muscle and bone.

He paints all night and then intermittently for the next few days. He paints feverishly, desperate to get some truth out onto the canvas, before it disappears from his mind. In between painting, he masturbates over pornographic videos and magazines. This, unlike reading, watching television or listening to music, does not interfere with the images and feelings that come to him. Like spirit manifesting at a séance, a life slowly seeps into the studio and onto Billy's canvas, conjured from the other side.

§

'Billy? It's Jamie. Are you there…? Hello? Where are you? I've left you so many messages… Sorry I didn't make it on Thursday. Work has gone crazy. I'll come and see you tomorrow. Anyway, please call me back. Anyone would think you're having an affair.'

§

Billy enters The Palais against a wall of sound and a backdrop of laser lights, dry ice and strobes. The soaring, woven fabric of music is perforated by a hair-raising pizzicato. Underneath breathes a floor of raging strings and an urgent drumbeat, threaded with the howl of synthesised sound.

An old recycled theatre-turned-party-venue opens out into the dress circle, from which, as he reaches the over-hanging balcony, Billy observes the mass of revellers on the dance floor below. Topless men, dancing in neon combat trousers, hang out of elaborately moulded rococo boxes on both sides of the decrepit theatre, hydrating themselves with water carried in illuminated shoulder holsters.

Billy looks down at the crowd moving together—each figure a cell of one giant animal, collectively pulsing and breathing as one.

He lifts up his camera. 'Fucking magical,' he says, aiming it into the crowd. He leans back against the edge of the balcony, craning his camera towards the upper circle, the gallery and right to the top where fingers of laser light stroke the ceiling of the gods. His E has already started to work. He recognises the signs this time: sweaty palms, tingling in the stomach, a slight rise in the heart-beat. Will Jamie join in? How will he explain? He can hardly say the old man upstairs gave them to him.

By the time Jamie arrives, Billy is swaying on the edge of the dance floor. He can feel beads of sweat on his forehead, heat in his cheeks. Jamie stares at him through the fronds of laser light passing between them.

'Hello, boyfriend,' Jamie says, and touches Billy's short cropped hair with his fingertips. 'What have you been doing today?'

Billy flexes his biceps.

'You're so unbelievably gay.'

'And you have a problem with that because…'

They both laugh. 'I spoke to Mum earlier. She sends her love.'

Billy nods. He's not in the frame of mind to talk about Gloria.

Jamie looks great, if a little over dressed. 'Aren't you warm?' Billy asks, undoing the buttons of Jamie's shirt.

'It's cool outside,' Jamie says. 'And obviously, I'm not as worked up as you.'

Worked up? Billy bites his lip. Can Jamie tell just by looking?

They are jostled by other clubbers, a crowd of toothy grins. The music gradually gains pace, becoming steadily more intense. They dance, smiling at each other—smoke blasts at them from the side of the auditorium. Billy looks at the faces around him, noticing the dewy eyes of the crowd. Is that how he looks? Billy closes his eyes. Their bodies move with the music, like swimmers moving with the swell of an ocean. There's a drum roll and a single synthesized note comes in, chasing a racing melody beneath the drums. The note is lasting in duration, curling gradually upward in pitch until it floats high above all else, over the drums, over the strings, higher and higher. Jamie is pushed closer to Billy with the surge. They stare deep into each other. Closer. Ecstasy rushes through Billy's brain. 'Fucking amazing,' he yells. Everyone's hands are in the air, tracing the note getting higher, more and more piercing. When Billy opens his eyes, they are almost touching. He looks up, reaching with his hands, as if the note has materialized in solid form, visible to his eyes, rising with the laser light. As the sonic shape reaches its apex, high above the dance floor there is a huge explosion of bass and a flash of firework. Glitter explodes over the crowd. There is a moment's silence as they, too, are travelling through the air after that single note. As Billy's mind reaches solid ground, the beat kicks in again and everyone goes wild—

'Having a good time?' Billy shouts, struggling to make himself heard over the pounding trance music.

'Yeah, thanks.' Jamie nods, looking ever so slightly unimpressed. They are not on the same level. Billy knows he's been found out. 'Have you taken something?' Jamie asks.

Billy winces and points to his ears pretending to be unable to hear. Jamie leans into him and shouts, loud enough to deafen him. 'You look like your jaw has been wired.' He hands Billy a packet of chewing gum.

'Thanks,' he says, gaining awareness for his grinding teeth, muscles bulging in his cheeks. He takes a piece of gum and hands the packet back to Jamie. He cocks his head and nods to the club. 'I bet your mum would love it here.'

Jamie throws his eyes up. 'I don't think you'd find my mother getting off her tits in a place like this.'

He breaks off and wanders to the bar. In a minute or so he returns with another gin and tonic. He looks a little nervous and slightly out of place. 'You okay?' Billy asks.

'I'm fine,' assures Jamie.

Billy reaches into his pocket, discreetly turning away from him for a moment. He feels around for a pill and presses one into his palm. Retrieving his hand, he holds out a downturned fist to Jamie. 'Take it.'

Jamie shakes his head. 'Not my thing,' he says. 'Where did you get them from?'

'Never mind where I got them from. Come on, take it,' Billy encourages, finding Jamie's reserve cute and slightly sexy.

'Is it safe?'

'Your mother's not watching now.'

Jamie eventually moves closer, cupping his hand beneath Billy's. Billy smiles, lets the pill drop into Jamie's hand and watches him slip the tiny white tablet between his lips. Billy pushes another pill into his own mouth. 'I wish I could feel like this forever!' he says, feeling his eyelids becoming heavy and slightly droopy.

'Forever?' Jamie asks. There is a slight look of horror in his eyes.

Billy punches him affectionately on the shoulder. 'Forever!' he says.

§

They have been dancing for some time before Billy realises Jamie is as dewy eyed and loose-limbed as himself; as if they've suddenly woken from a dream, they stare longingly into each other. Billy peels Jamie from his now damp shirt and threads it through the belt of his jeans. He rubs him affectionately on the stomach, touching the hair around Jamie's navel.

Aroused, longing to kiss him, Billy pulls him through the

crowd and leads him, rather inelegantly, upstairs. On the gallery, Billy opens the door to the gents' toilet and finds a dimly lit room crowded with men. 'Where are you taking me?' complains Jamie and they bundle in.

The small room has urinals along one wall, two cubicles and a very low ceiling. This is not a *toilet*. The door closes behind them. The room becomes a little darker. Billy can just make out a group of topless men at the back. There is the sound of muffled music from the gallery and the sounds of men moving around in the dark, breathing, whispering, the shuffle of shoes on a dirty, sticky floor. The two of them lean against the wall for a moment, waiting for their eyes to adjust to the gloom.

'How long does this take to wear off?' Jamie whispers.

'Stop worrying. Just relax.'

'But I've got work tomorrow.'

Two men grope each other, playing with each other's nipples, kissing passionately: 'Action Men' types pumped with steroids with beards and army style haircuts. Billy can't stop staring. In his head he gives the guys names. The first one, *Bluto*, reminds him of the character from *Popeye*. This guy reaches for the other's hand. Let's call him *Bruno*, thinks Billy. Bluto pulls his hand and places it flat on his own flies, encouraging Bruno to rub the fabric where his cock lies beneath. Undoing the zip of Bluto's camouflage combat trousers, his mate's fingers probe inside, pop open the buttons and draw out the flesh that lies beneath. Bruno caresses him with big hands until he becomes longer, harder. Billy trembles, watching intently as Bluto loosens his combats and pushes them over his buttocks, revealing more flesh. His mound of neatly trimmed pubic hair is slightly damp, stuck to his flesh in tiny curls.

He looks over at Billy and Jamie, hungrily. Only an arm's reach away, he breathes deeply through his nostrils, biting his bottom lip. He nods, questioning—*do you want to join in?* Bruno gasps as Bluto tweaks the studs of his nipples again. An ecstatic moan comes from the back of the room as someone is penetrated. More men, on the prowl, enter, eyes searching the obscurity. Men huddle in corners, snorting bumps of white powder from the ends of door keys.

Orange dots of glowing cigarette ends float around like fireflies in the dark. Condensation drips from the low ceiling. One after another, men enter the little toilet until Billy and Jamie are pressed together, flesh against flesh. Billy feels hands groping. He catches eyes, dilated, the room awash with Ecstasy. Further in, Bluto and Bruno are swallowing capfuls of something—compounds that might be found in Albert's book. He moves deeper in. Bruno is kneeling in front of Bluto, tonguing him, making him moan loudly. Billy can't wait any longer. He turns so that Jamie's face is closer to his. Parts of them touch—knees, a shoulder, Billy's finger-tips against Jamie's snake-hips. At first, they are too close for eye contact. Billy grabs Jamie and kisses him hard on the lips. He responds. They are suddenly in a clinch, hands all over each other. He holds him close. His tongue dances with Jamie's. The wetness of their spit mixes together. Jamie's mouth moves over Billy's neck, his wet tongue sliding on skin, across his throat, down his nipples. He traces circles around them, making Billy gasp. Billy's hands are undoing Jamie's jeans. A few strokes on his cock and Jamie whispers, 'Stop,' squeezing his bare shoulders, hands on his tattoos. But Billy won't stop. He races away—his mouth thrusting. 'Stop, now!'

Unreal. They are there in the dark, men standing in circles, jerking off, sucking, fucking, fingering, kissing, while the rest of London goes about its business. Billy watches as Bluto's large hands reach forward for Jamie's nipples, pinching each in between thumb and forefinger, twisting gently. Jamie gasps and falls gently back against Bluto's chest, happy to let it all happen. Billy looks at them, greedily. Bluto takes a foil wrapper out of his combats, winks at Bruno, and nods towards Jamie. The waiting is worst. Bruno takes the condom and moves behind Jamie, back to the wall. He grabs him by the waist, a hand on Jamie's groin, bends him over, pulls him firmly against him. Jamie bucks as Bruno pushes deep inside him.

§

When Billy reaches across the bedspread, Jamie is not there. A vague memory comes back to him—Jamie getting into a cab and going home to his own place. That bloody job always comes first.

Eventually, Billy rises from his slumber; he goes straight to the half-finished canvas on the easel next to the desk. The first thing on his mind is the portrait. The features are there, protruding like bone and muscle beneath flesh. He has yet to add the vital marks that will give it genuine personality.

He leans over his desk and studies his pale, ghastly face in the mirror. He touches the skin with the tips of his fingers, tentatively, as if it belongs to someone else. He feels his way around his skull, his cheekbones, his jawbone, probes his eye sockets. He breathes in again, deeply, recalling the scent of lavender filling his nostrils.

Feverishly, his eyes move across the back wall of images. He reaches, accidentally scattering a pile of cuttings, models torn from magazines. A book on 'Screen Legends' catches his eye, photography of famous actors in films. He flicks through it and begins to feel something. The air feels thicker, more conductive and there is an essence, like low voltage electricity. This is how it finds its way to him. He lifts a paintbrush from a glass jar and begins to rub it against the canvas. He remembers the loneliness of the old man. He sees Albert in his mind's eye. And then he sees this other man. The motion of his wrist provokes a link from the paintbrush to his brain and from his brain to wherever it is he sources the images from—*out there*. It's a meditation aided by the smell of linseed oil and turpentine that saturates the air. That is how the images come. No model required.

The oils on his palette are still wet from his last session. Connected, he dips his paintbrush in several colours, umbers and siennas, a bit of ultramarine, to daub and blend on the canvas. He mixes a skin tone, a touch of green here, a bit of red there. The picture gains clarity as he places a highlight on the forehead, a sparkle in the eyes, a crease between the nostril and the curl of the lip. He builds up the layers of flesh and breathes life into the emerging portrait. There it is, forming, changing and reforming before his eyes—the face of a man he's never met before.

He paints until he is satisfied with how far he's gone. He puts the paintbrush and palette down and stands back from the portrait, nodding agreeably. Then he walks to the mirror, stares at his ghostly reflection. Dark rings surround his popping eyes, pupils so dilated that there is very little of the iris left. His own changed face fascinates him, skin waxy and clammy. How do I feel? he thinks. Maybe there is the slight feeling that something is missing. A memory—something he can't think of... not quite there anymore, but he doesn't let it bother him. He shuffles into his tiny kitchen, to make tea, eats some chocolate from the fridge and then heads back to bed.

§

Billy leans against Albert's upstairs doorframe. "Ello 'ello 'ello.'

He makes Albert jump. 'Jesus! Darling Boy.'

Billy holds Albert's door key in the air. 'You want to be more careful' he says. 'I found it in the keyhole at the bottom of the stairs.'

'Bloody hell, I must have forgotten,' Albert says, touching his forehead with the palm of one hand. 'One of these days it really is going to be the local plod standing there.'

'And you say there's nothing wrong with your memory.'

Albert is sitting on the Chesterfield, in front of a small set of weighing scales, on the coffee table. He is weighing some sort of brown mess into little plastic bags.

'A policeman's dream, this place. You could go down for five lifetimes!' Billy says.

'Yes. So you should be careful what you say about me to other people. Concrete slippers wouldn't suit you. I'm an unlikely drug-dealer. Small operation. That's why I get away with it.'

Billy strides into the room and throws himself down on the Chesterfield.

Albert sits looking at him. 'You're sprightly today. Thought you went out last night?'

'I did. Been in bed most of the day,' Billy rubs sleep from his eyes.

'You still feeling that nice fuzziness?' Albert enthuses, as if speaking about jelly and ice-cream.

'Yeah. Even now.'

'Hmm. Bona doobs, those ones. You look nice. Tailored short trousers suit you,' Albert says, glancing at his legs. He sits forward and organises the items on the table.

'Thanks.' Billy slips his red braces off his shoulders so they won't overstretch when he sits down. He looks at Albert's weighing scales. 'What are you doing?'

'A couple of orders. Strictly medicinal! A bit of dope for Mrs Jenkins' arthritis and mushrooms for Mr Carter's cluster head-aches.' Albert points to the small plastic bags.

'Cluster headaches? Billy is bemused.

'Like migraines, but worse,' Albert says. 'Very rare. And the medical industry offers no cure. But these seem to do the trick.'

'How can a mushroom cure a headache?' Billy asks, unbutton-ing the top buttons of his black shirt.

'These are magic,' Albert says, holding up one of the little bags and tapping it with a fingertip.

'Yes. I know what they are.'

'Psilocybin is the active ingredient in them, which becomes Psilocyn when it's metabolised in the body. This cures the headache.'

'How?' Billy persists.

'Do you really need to know how?'

'No. I suppose not.'

'Well, let's leave it there then.' Albert scrapes up the rest of the brown mess into a plastic re-sealable bag. Looking directly at Billy again, he says, 'You shouldn't really see any of this, you know.'

Billy leans over and kisses him gently on the lips. 'I thought we were going to look at my work?'

§

The entrance to the arts trust, where Billy works part-time and used to have a studio, is hidden from view, down a narrow private side street, off Kingsland Road in Shoreditch. He had to give up the studio but some of his paintings are still stored there. Through a pair of wrought iron gates, Albert follows Billy in between the two nineteenth century factory buildings, the gallery on the left, and a rabbit warren of studios on the right, home to more than fifty artists. The street is lit from above by a zigzagged string of coloured light bulbs.

'Do you know, I've lived in this area nearly all my life and I never knew all this was here,' Albert says, quick stepping behind Billy.

Billy leads Albert up a wooden staircase on the outside of the building. At the top of the scaffold they reach a door which leads into the studio. Inside, his large-scale canvasses lean in groups against the wall of the lofty room. Some smaller ones are collected in boxes, waiting to be collected, now that a new artist has moved in.

Billy flips through some of the canvasses. He and Albert stand next to each other, looking at the work, a closeness between them—no boundary where one's personal space ends and the other's begins. Their hips are almost together, their hands discreetly touching. Another sort of substance is at work here. Billy can feel a chemistry between them.

'Well, I am stunned, Darling Boy.'

The images of faces, chin to forehead, like those infamous 'choker' shots from old film-noir movies, create a dramatic, claustrophobic effect. Each is a snap-shot from Billy's life: moments that could have been lost in the blink of an eye, now immortalised on canvas. 'I managed to attract an art dealer just as I was finishing art school. It meant that I could continue painting for some time.'

Albert looks at him, the way an older man sometimes looks at a younger man, full of lust. Billy can't quite decide whether it is nostalgia or envy in his eyes, but there is definitely lust.

'I'm intrigued, Billy. What's your motivation? Why do you paint?'

Billy pauses for a moment before answering. 'It's cathartic, I suppose.' He pulls several paintings out for Albert to view more closely: scenes of the lawlessness of school, the wasteland of childhood. He remembers how he never really fitted in. 'I paint in an attempt to understand my world.'

'So it's therapy for you?'

'No. Therapy is therapy. Painting is painting. It's not the same thing. Painting helps me to explore something. I can pick up a fragment of my life, look at it from every angle. I can explore every nuance there is within it. And then I can put it down and say, 'I know that now. I can leave it alone.' That's why some of them look so similar. That's me, revisiting, getting closer to the truth. I paint to find out who I am.'

Albert nods encouragingly. 'And have you succeeded?'

'Don't know.' Billy shrugs and stuffs his hands in his pockets again.

'Well, let's hope you don't get too close, or you'll lose your reason to paint.' Albert smiles, studying the images. 'I mean, Darling Boy, you must paint. Every minute available, you must do it.'

'I am painting.' Billy thinks of the portrait he's been working on in the back room. 'You've given me a new lease of life.'

'Really?'

'Yes. It's my best work to date, I'd say.'

Albert's transfixed by one particular canvas. 'It's obvious who this one is.' Billy smiles at the picture of the young boy around the age of five or six years, wide-eyed, deep and black, surrounded by pale luminous unblemished white skin. The wells of his eyes so deep you could fall into them.

'I thought I knew everything then—who I was, where I was going.'

'And now?' Albert asks.

'Lost.'

He wishes now that Albert hadn't seen this painting. It makes him feel exposed and vulnerable. There is a whole life that Albert doesn't know about—his life with Jamie. He doesn't want to talk about any of this. He enjoys his secret time with Albert but his other life is becoming more and more difficult to hide. Thinking about who he was when he was at school fills him with shame. Billy can feel a tug in his body. Jesus, he could murder a drink.

Albert moves closer to the canvases to observe the brushwork. 'You know, Billy, I think we're actually born somebody. And then that somebody sometimes gets lost along the way. Sometimes people can spend the rest of their lives looking for that person. At the end of the day, we're all lost.' Albert nudges him on the shoulder and smiles. 'To look at you in this painting is to look at something from another universe. You've captured the essence of yourself so well. There's something very special in your eyes.'

§

At ten o'clock, Billy and Albert are entering the upstairs flat. They avoid turning on the lights. The room, while partially dusted with moonlight, remains to the larger extent in shadow. Moving across the room, Billy threads a trail of smoke through the air with a joint he's smoking. He stands in his favourite place beside the chaise longue in the open window. The warm and unmoving night air supports the smoke so that it is suspended like a grey phantasm, only very slowly dissipating. He watches Albert remove his Panama and his jacket and throw them on the Chesterfield. Then unbuttoning his shirt at the neck, Albert walks forward into the moonlight. 'Be careful with that stuff, Billy,' he says, solemnly.

'Just a bit of puff, Albert. You can't be worried about that.' Billy coughs on smoke.

Albert's face catches the moonlight. Pinpoints of light sparkle in his deep-set eyes. 'You're in the business of chronicling the past, and the nature of most drugs is to erase it from memory.'

Billy stares at him through the darkness. He offers the last bit to him, the last ember glowing orange in the dark. Albert takes the joint, draws deeply on what's left and flicks the stub into the street. Billy turns slowly away from the window and steps forward, knowing Albert will only see him cast into silhouette. They stand frozen like the smoke in the air, a dream, two men sharing the same room, something growing in the space between them.

'Give me a match,' Albert says. Billy hands him the lighter from his pocket and Albert moves gently, lighting and positioning candles around the room. 'What are you, Billy Monroe?' Albert asks. Billy waits, says nothing, detecting the room changing shape, growing brighter. 'You're my angel, from another world,' Albert finishes.

'Maybe I can give you a dream,' Billy says, huskily. He thinks for a moment about the painting downstairs and smiles. 'What are *you*, Albert Power?'

'A man,' he answers, simply and deliberately. 'Nothing more.' He stops in the middle of the room. The candlelight dances on his face.

'What am I doing with a man?' Billy says, hearing the tone of satisfaction in his own voice. 'What's happening here, Albert? What are we doing?' He moves closer to him.

'You're having an affair,' Albert says. Billy can see him smiling in the moonlight. 'With an older man!'

'Hardly an affair,' Billy says. 'I'm not married.'

'It's a secret, though. Is it not?'

'Only because *you* want it to be.'

'It will keep its magic that way. But it *is* an affair.'

'Of sorts.'

'Better to avoid too many labels. They only lend themselves to the prosaic, the mundane.' Now they are close—almost touching. 'Do you mind that, Darling Boy?'

'I don't care what you call it. All boils down to the same thing,' Billy says.

'What's that?'

'Sex.'

61

'Our world, Billy! Here, we can do whatever we want. No one else need ever know about it. They'd want us to be 'boyfriends', go to parties—all that palaver. You don't want that. You don't want to be seen *out* with an old man.' Albert tilts his head.

Well, that's a relief, thinks Billy. He doesn't want to think about it. 'Do you have anything to drink, Albert?'

Albert raises an eyebrow. He's silent for a moment and then he says something that takes Billy by surprise. 'Don't you think you're drinking quite a lot?'

Billy feels himself become defensive. 'Why do you say that?'

'Darling boy, far be it from me to judge but... what are you trying to escape?'

Billy thinks about the secrets on top of secrets that he's been keeping. He thinks about how duplicitous he has been to both Jamie and Albert. His lies will catch up with him. He knows this. The idea clenches inside his gut like a fist.

Disconnected from his thoughts, Billy's hands rise to Albert's shirt buttons. He undoes them one by one and pulls his shirt off. Under moonlight, Albert's skin glows like phosphorous. Billy watches Albert's hungry, luminous eyes moving down over his body. He can feel Albert's fingers trace the patterns of his tattoos.

He can't hide his surprise at the firmness of Albert's body.

'What were you imagining, Darling Boy? Rolls of fat?' Albert's hands are suddenly all over Billy, sliding across the curves of his muscles. It feels to Billy as if there are many hands on him—stroking, caressing, probing every inch of him, inside and outside—many hands, many mouths, many bodies. Now, Albert is behind him, pressing himself against him, pressing into the damp space between his firm, round arse cheeks.

They kiss, pulling clothes from each other. In moments, they are naked.

§

Then comes a speechless moment when all movement ceases. Billy feels Albert resting, still inside him. They say nothing. What is there to say? Words are meaningless and only serve to make matters awkward. Slowly and gently, he feels Albert pull away, kiss him on his neck. Albert walks into the kitchen. There's the sound of him clicking the kettle on. He returns, sending the beaded curtain skittering, and throws Billy a kitchen towel to mop up with.

Slipping away into a trance, a residue of ecstasy still working in Billy's brain, his eyes roll back into his head. Moments later, he senses Albert come back into the room and then his head being lifted into Albert's lap. 'I've made Earl Grey.'

'Got any more of those pills?'

'You don't need pills,' Albert says, stroking his hair.

'For another time.'

'A likely story. Dependency is not a road you want to go down.'

'Don't be daft.'

Albert shrugs. 'I can get you whatever you want, Darling Boy.'

Billy grins. 'Now that I am an object of your desire.'

'Drink your tea and then sleep, Darling Boy.'

§

Lying on Billy's bed, Jamie holds *The Complete Guide to Recreational Psychoactives* upright on his chest, in one hand, and twiddles a set of keys between the fingers of the other—the keys to the flat which Billy had given him.

Billy watches from the foot of the bed and at the same time, struggles to fix the television. There's a documentary about sex on Channel Four that he wants to watch. Pizza and shit TV—hangover cure. Jamie, flicking through the book, stops at random pages, reading out loud. 'Ketamine—a psychedelic, sedative drug, used recreationally to induce a state of mild disequilibrium and dissociative anaesthesia... street name—Special K... LSD—d-lysergic acid diethylamide, used in transcendental practices, psycho-nautical trips... most commonly known as Acid or Trips...' He pauses, closes the book momentarily and looks at the cover. 'Where did you get this book?' he asks. 'It's got everything in here.'

'It's been lying around for ages,' Billy says. 'I borrowed it from the guy upstairs a few months ago.'

'What? Albert? That old fella?'

'Yes. He invited me in for a cup of tea in the summer, when I was off work.' Billy continues to fiddle with the TV set, trying not to look Jamie in the eye.

'You never said you'd actually been in there?' Jamie says.

'I keep meaning to give it back to him but I haven't seen him recently.'

Jamie looks back at the book. 'Crystal meth—a powerful euphoric stimulant, with a reputation for being one of the most dangerous drugs because of its addictive and destructive qualities…' Jamie snaps the books shut. 'Funny sort of thing for an old man to have around the flat.'

Billy blows out a heavy sigh. 'Jesus, I've got a headache.'

'I'm not surprised with all that socialising with clients that you do.'

'Wooing a buyer is easier to do with a glass of wine in my hand.' Billy bites and then instantly regrets it.

'You're in a funny mood today. What are you hiding?' Jamie says. There's a seriousness to his voice.

'Bloody thing!' Billy says, punching buttons on the television, deliberately changing the subject. 'It's stuck on BBC2.' He gives the television a good thump on top and, 'Voila!', Channel Four, just in time for the sex.

Jamie finally stands up, demonstratively, with the book in his hands. Billy braces himself. 'This reminds me of when we were in that bedsit in Camden. You got the sack from that job at that Belgian fashion company,' Jamie says. 'You'd been drinking *then* as well. Do you remember?' he says with an accusing tone in his voice. 'You got pissed at one of their staff dos and embarrassed yourself.'

Billy stands, flinches almost. 'What are you trying to say?'

'You never were any good at lying,' Jamie says.

Billy knows he has to tread carefully. There's something about

65

the way Jamie is speaking that sounds both sympathetic and yet at the same time very final.

'You carried on getting up and leaving the flat at eight in the morning every day to make me believe you were going to work, while all along you were desperately trying to find a new job. Then when you did find work, you told me you were moving to something better and that the *old* job wasn't your thing. You thought you could pull the wool over my eyes, but I can see through you, Billy Monroe. You withdrew money from the joint account three times in that month.'

Billy drops the TV remote on the bed suddenly feeling very exposed. He wasn't stupid enough to think that had all gone unnoticed. 'I'm sorry.'

'Sorry?' Jamie asks, sardonically. 'What have you got to be sorry for?'

The question hangs in the air like an accusation waiting to bite him. 'I lead you a right life, don't I? I'm not the greatest person to live with.'

'We don't live together. *Yet.*' Jamie says. 'Which reminds me— there are some forms from the solicitor back at home for you to sign.'

Billy is not used to Jamie having the upper hand. 'I've given you the run around,' he says. 'And I'm sorry.'

'All part of being in a relationship, isn't it? I don't give up so easily.' Jamie turns from Billy, perhaps a little overwhelmed, perhaps a tear in his eye. He looks back at the book. 'It says here that you can synthesise Crystal meth in your own kitchen. You ever do this stuff?'

'Jesus! Jamie! What do you take me for? That's made of drain cleaner.'

'Only asking. No need to bite my head off.'

'Will you put that thing down! We're meant to be watching this together.'

§

Travelling on the bus, from the Curzon cinema in Soho back to Shoreditch, Billy insists on sitting upstairs, right at the front. He's enjoying making Albert feel uncomfortable by resting his head on his shoulder and discreetly touching his leg.

'Don't,' Albert says, swatting him away like an insect.

Billy loves plaguing him. Stepping off the bus, he pinches his arse.

'You mustn't do that,' Albert says, as they walk along the pavement.

For all his years, Albert is unreservedly reserved. 'Mustn't what?' Billy asks.

'I don't want you to do that in public,' Albert replies, walking into the fish and chip shop.

'It's the twenty-first century! No-one cares if I touch you or not.'

'*I care*. I'm not used to that sort of thing. Please don't do it.'

Moments later they're sharing a portion of cod and chips on their way down Columbia Road. 'The nights are drawing in,'

Albert remarks.

Billy laughs. 'Albert, it's October.'

'It's colder, too.'

'It's been freezing for ages,' Billy says. 'Did you miss September?'

'The months have flown by and I hadn't noticed. Anyway, what did you think of the film? I thought Marlon Brando set the screen aflame.'

Billy nods, mouth full of greasy fish. 'Vivien Leigh, porcelain doll of the silver screen. Divine.'

They are nearly at The Royal Oak when Albert looks at him sideways and says, 'We'll just go in here for a drink. That alright?'

Billy frowns at him suspiciously and discards a clump of oily paper and fish batter in a rubbish bin. 'If you want to. I thought you were keen to get back?'

'*Molly* bar,' Albert says. He shivers and points up at the tattered old rainbow flag above the doors, flapping in the breeze. 'My round,' he says, entering the public house. It's a real spit'n'sawdust kind of place with a mixed clientele. Not the world Billy's used to. Its after-hours reputation often attracts a *morning after* crowd. He recognises faces from the art set of Hoxton and Shoreditch, and there's a sprinkling of unbefitting queer punters. And you're required to be over the age of eighteen just to look at some of them. Billy stands behind Albert, while he orders two pints of lager. Albert spots someone he recognizes on the other side of the bar. He raises a hand and waves. 'Hello, Eric.'

Eric nods and comes over carrying a pint of lager. He's unshaven, in a polo shirt and tracksuit bottoms. He and Albert shake hands. He has tattoos of German Shepherd dogs on his forearms. He points to a booth, near a frosted glass window.

'We'll join you in a second,' Albert says. 'A top up, Eric?'

'Nah, I'm alright, fella!' Eric says, holding up his half-finished pint. Billy watches him walk over to the booth, taking lots of very little steps, really quickly, shoulders pivoting quickly forwards and backwards, looking really busy. Billy smiles to himself, re-membering he has seen Eric before, washing his car. He waits for Albert to pay and then follows him, carrying the drinks.

'I wondered when you were gonna troll on down here,' Eric says. 'Ain't seen you in a while, Albert.'

'This is Billy,' Albert says, slipping into the booth, opposite Eric.

'Nice trade, Fungus!' Eric says, looking at Albert and then winking at Billy.

'Mind your billingsgate,' Albert says, sharply.

'Alright, fella?' Eric says, extending his hand towards Billy.

'Good, thanks.' They shake hands. 'And yourself?'

'Grand!' Eric says. Then looking back at Albert he asks, 'How's business, old fruit?'

'Picking up. Thanks for putting those film guys in touch with me. Wanted stuff for a wrap party. No pun intended.'

Eric gets a cigarette packet out of his pocket and places it in the middle of the table. 'Usual.'

'Eight?' Albert asks.

'Yeah.'

Billy watches Albert, sitting quietly for a moment, drinking his beer, perusing the room. Everybody is minding their own business. He wonders why Albert is being so surreptitious. These people don't give a shit who or what is going down. Then, as Albert discreetly picks up the cigarette packet, he flips open the top and checks inside. He nods and puts the cigarette packet in his breast pocket. He smiles at Eric and says, 'This stuff is bona.'

'Ya never fail to please, fella!'

Albert drinks more beer before looking around the room again. He reaches into his other breast pocket to fetch out an identical cigarette packet and places it in front of Eric who picks it up quickly. He taps it gently on the table, before stuffing it into his pocket. 'Right,' Eric starts, 'I'm off to slap me onk.'

Billy acknowledges the hilarious translation for *powder my nose* and smiles.

'Have a nice time, mate.'

Albert nods. 'We must be off.' He looks at Billy and nods towards the door.

'Hang on. I haven't finished my drink yet,' Billy says and gulps down his lager.

'Cheers, fella.' Eric smiles. 'You be in next week?'

Outside, under the frayed rainbow flag, Billy shakes his head at Albert.

'Just a bit of business.' Albert strides off down the street.

'That was *it*? Christ, how much did you take?'

'Three hundred and fifty quid.'

'For a bit of sniff?'

'A man has to eat.'

'He's in the neighbourhood. Why didn't you pop round?'

'Some people like to hide in plain sight.'

'Albert, have you been carrying drugs around with you all day?'

'Yes.'

At the corner of Laburnum Road they turn and walk briskly down to the maisonettes. Billy touches Albert on the bottom.

'Billy, do behave yourself!' Albert hisses.

§

Billy stands in socks, vest and boxers, in the doorway between Albert's kitchen and front room, tangled and posturing in the coloured glass droplets of beaded curtain—a pastiche of an LA showgirl. In front of him Albert is sprawled on the chaise longue before the open window.

Drawing on a spliff, the old man looks as if he has sunk deep into an oceanic mind. 'I know *that* face,' Billy says, but Albert doesn't stir. He untangles himself from the beads and moves nearer to the window. 'Albert?'

Albert looks up. 'Oh, Billy. Miles away.' Billy touches him on the shoulder. 'What is it Darling Boy?'

'Remember when we were together on that first night?'

'Yes.'

'Just before I left, you were talking about another man. You said he painted that portrait of you.' Billy points to the painting on the wall.

71

'I remember.'

'He was important to you, yeah?'

'Darling Boy, he was the love of my life.'

'You were *together*?'

Albert's eyes smile. 'I met him when I was twenty. We knew each other for thirty years. He died.'

'I'm sorry.'

'Sometimes I get mixed up and I think you are *him*.'

Billy smiles. 'How did he die?'

'The secrecy drove him mad in the end. He committed suicide.'

'Albert. That's just awful.'

'Well, anyway, that's past now.' Albert lifts his arm and hands the spliff to Billy.

Billy is thinking about his palette, about Prussian blue and magenta. 'Odd question.' he says, drawing on the spliff. 'What colour were his eyes?'

§

'You've not been painting?' Albert asks.

'I've slowed down.'

'Oh, this *is* bad news.' Albert is lighting tea lights one after another and placing them on the floor around him. He takes another handful from the bag that Billy brought from downstairs, when the power went off.

'I just want to walk away from it all,' Billy says, dropping his lighter on the floor and sipping from his glass of red wine. Sitting comfortably on the floor of Albert's living room without electrical light, they are surrounded by hundreds of the little tea-lights. *Hundreds* of them! They have transformed the room into a candlelit grotto. The whole street is out.

Gradually, from the blackness, the room has grown light and the walls are alive, flickering with candlelight. 'I love what you're wearing, Darling Boy,' Albert says, eventually, now that it's bright enough to see. The blood red shirt that Billy had worn earlier to meet his art dealer is shot through and embroidered with silver, reflecting the candlelight. He traces a finger over the glinted thread. It's on the tip of his tongue to divulge that it was a gift from Jamie, but stops himself at the last second. He doesn't want Jamie creeping into his time with Albert—the job, the flat hunting. He should message him.

Aside from the canvas he's been working on downstairs, he's not been doing much in the way of painting. He's very down. Even Albert's drugs don't seem to cheer him up anymore. But with Albert it is glamorous alchemy. 'What we do together helps me recharge my batteries. And then I go back to my other life.'

Albert's eyes drop to the floor. 'It can't always be like this.'

'Why not? No one understands what we have together.'

'You should probably be with someone your own age.' Candlelight flickers across Albert's lined face, betraying sadness. 'You should be with someone with similar ambitions. Not wasting your time with an old goat like me.'

'Don't say that,' Billy says. 'It's like we've known each other for hundreds of years.'

'Well, of course that's the *only* explanation,' Albert agrees. 'Perhaps even *thousands.*'

'That's maybe why we feel we know each other so well. And we'll *always* know each other. Till the end of time.'

Billy sighs a deep, resigned sort of sigh and stares at all the tealights. They make him feel like he is deep underground, in a cave or a mine. 'Have you heard of Lapis Lazuli?' he asks.

'It's a colour, in paint, isn't it?'

'It's a pigment, made from crushed gemstones. The deepest, bluest, fairy tale blue you ever saw. It's a splendid colour—regal. Its sparkling quality is because of the tiny particles of pyrite within it, twinkling like microscopic stars. Created a gazillion years ago. So you could say it's been around forever. It's been used for thousands of years in many paintings. Really expensive and considered very powerful, and now it is so rare that it can only be found in these mines in Afghanistan, deep underground. Can you imagine those gemstones have been there for a real long time? Like *you* and *me.* That's how I felt when I met you. I felt like I'd found something so rare, and so indelible. This stuff doesn't fade, you see. You take a look at all those paintings of the Virgin Mary in the National Gallery. The backgrounds have paled, but her robes are still royal blue. And when the light hits it from a certain angle, it glows. Lapis Lazuli.'

'Remarkable, Darling boy!'

Billy lets his head drop back against the arm of the Chesterfield. 'I need the next show to really work. I need to sell a painting, Albert. Fuck! I need to sell lots of them.'

'You won't sell them if you don't paint them.'

§

'You look like shit, Darling boy!'

Billy looks up from his big pad of paper on the wooden floor of Albert's living room. 'I know what I look like,' he says. Even though it is getting dim the lights stay off, while he works. Today, he's making a drawing of Albert in charcoal and deep blue Indian ink. His hand moves over the paper methodically, meticulously recording the vital truths that make Albert who he is: a broad brow, hooded eyes, a slight longness of the tooth, elegant nose.

'Are you eating properly?' Albert asks.

I wish everyone would just get off my fucking case, Billy thinks. He traces Albert's jawline with a brush of indigo and smudges the charcoal around his nostrils. He exchanges the charcoal for a piece of white oil pastel and adds highlights under Albert's eyes.

'You need to get more sleep. You know what will happen. I told you...'

'Yeah, yeah,' Billy holds up a hand to halt him. 'Don't give me the third degree.'

Albert is sitting on the Chesterfield, wearing a deep green shirt with a cravat the colour of red wine. He holds a vertical posture. Arching his back regally, he says, 'How do I look?'

Billy sucks the end of his pencil for a minute. 'Hungry.'

Albert laughs. Billy moves his sketchbook aside and stands up.

75

'Finished?' Albert asks.

'For now.'

'We should eat,' Albert says, stretching his arms and arching his back.

'You didn't spend long on that. I thought you were trying to persevere with the work?'

Billy gets his jacket from on the back of the door. He scratches his head, fiddles with his belt buckle, rubs his eyes, avoiding further questions.

'Going?' Albert asks.

'No.' Billy reaches into the top pocket of his jacket and goes back to the coffee table. He kneels, empties out white powder onto the glass surface from a paper wrap made of a National Lottery play slip. 'Want a line?'

'No,' Albert says, folding his arms.

'Mind if *I* have one?'

'Whatever limbers you up.' Albert chews his bottom lip.

'Stop being so pious.'

Billy quickly chops a line, rolls up a twenty-pound note and snorts it. The cocaine hits the membrane at the back of his nose and crackles behind his eyes. In a moment he feels the gentle high coming on, the quickening of his heartbeat, a slight heat at the temples, a tingle in the belly. He moves to sit next to Albert.

'Where did you get that from?' Albert asks.

'From your bureau,' Billy says without looking up.

Albert loosens his shirt and removes the cravat. He places it over the arm of the Chesterfield. 'Well I can't fault you for honesty. I didn't say you could help yourself.'

'You said yourself, it goes off if you keep it too long,' Billy says, pointing at the coke with his credit card.

'Well I won't be needing it much longer.'

'What?' Billy says and continues to move the charlie around the glass surface with the credit card. He drags it into straight lines. Then, seeing the imperfections in form and length, scratches them around, obsessively adjusting, the way he might straighten a tie.

'The big clean up. *Gentrification!*' Albert says.

'What you mean is—some geezer has moved in on your patch at The Oak.'

'Selling second class gear, I might add,' Albert spits. 'It's going to be a gastropub.'

Billy knows he is just sore because someone saw an opening and took it. In the last few months, Albert's dealing has dropped off.

'I'm too old for this game,' Albert says. 'I'm getting out.'

This strikes Billy straight away. He looks directly at Albert. '*Can* you get out? Are you able to just walk away from it? Whoever it is you're selling for will lose a fortune.'

The skin around Albert's eyes tightens for a moment. 'That's *my* problem.' Then he waves a finger at Billy and then at the cocaine on the table. 'Billy, just how much of that stuff have you been doing?'

Billy feels him observing out of the corner of his eye. 'I don't think you should be judging me. You're the one who got me into this.'

'Now, hang on Billy. I didn't get you into anything.'

'You gave me my first ecstasy pill in this very room.'

'Oh, come on. You wanted to know what it felt like. I had some lying around. I didn't force your hand. And if I remember correctly, you gave quite a floorshow. A few pills, Billy. It's a bit different to you casually helping yourself to several grams of charlie.'

Billy moves the powder around, drawing it into long thin lines, tapping the edge of the credit card on the glass. He runs it across his tongue. Oh *whatever*, he thinks. 'Look, do you want a line or not?' He wipes the excess from the table and smudges it into his gums.

Albert looks up to the ceiling in a resigned sort of way and then leans over the table.

§

Wired. Riding on coke, Billy feels his desire for Albert grow stronger. There is that pull, in the tummy, like magnetism. 'Feels good? No?' Billy asks.

'Well, it's woken me up, if that's what you mean!' Albert rubs his nostril with a handkerchief. Moments later they are locked in each other's arms, struggling to remove clothes. Albert tears at Billy's shirt. They roll and fall against the leather. Breath on heated breath, they bend together, violently. Albert presses his mouth vampirously against Billy's neck. They are naked, two bodies burning. Billy loves Albert's older flesh. The more delicate parts of Albert's body are beautiful. He runs his hands over the greyness of his hair, the minor paunch of his belly, the sagginess around his thighs. Albert is by no means frail, but the differences between their bodies tantalises Billy. He notices their flesh a closer shade, now that he has much less of a tan. 'Wait! Let's have another.' Billy frantically scrapes together four more lines, powder scattering across the glass surface. He snorts two. 'Go on,' he urges.

'Not for me. Got to watch the ticker.' Billy allows himself to be pulled by Albert. He resists a little, playfully, and then he is upon Albert, muscles enveloping him, crushing him, snakelike, pushing his hardness against Albert's belly. They thrash like dragons fighting, cock rubbing against cock. Billy regains control and takes hold of them between a fist and stimulates them both as one. He sits up, astride Albert so that their balls nuzzle together. He bucks as Albert pushes a finger into his arse and rushes them towards the end. His eyes roll back beneath the lids.

'What do you want me to do?' Billy exhales, opening his eyes again.

'Cum on my face,' Albert says, looking up at him. Pinpoints of light sparkled in his eyes.

Billy isn't sure. Albert might be pushing him too far.

'Please.'

Billy feels himself suddenly more alert.

'Yes, now, quick!' Albert begs.

'Sure?'

'Yes.'

Billy shunts forward, his arse now above Albert's face. He feels the stubble from Albert's chin scratch his testicles. They work themselves to the end. Albert's wild eyes sparkle underneath him—a look of anguish on his face.

'You ready?'

'No, Billy. Not yet!'

'Now?'

'Keep going!' Albert says, frowning, resisting the pleasure. 'Ah... yes... *now!*' They let go. Abruptly, Billy explodes volcanically onto Albert's face. The *slap* sound of it stuns him, as if being shaken from a daydream. Albert appears equally stunned. 'Oh, yes... all that cum...' he growls, pleasurably. But after the first pump, there is more. It oozes from Billy like honeyed tree resin. 'Oh, Darling boy!' Albert looks up, curling his lip like a beast. Billy can't hide the fact that he's shocked. He shocked *himself*. Staring back, he knows some line has been crossed.

'What's wrong?' Albert asks. A smile dissipates with the semen running down his face.

'Nothing...' Billy tries to hide disgust, but he knows he's already made Albert feel vulnerable.

Albert sits up. 'What?'

'You look...'

'I *know* how I look.' He touches semen on his face. 'Excuse me, for a moment.'

Billy gets off, unable to speak. He knows Albert will be angry. More than that. Upset. Why this, now? Why his childish, antiseptic reaction towards sex? Albert stands up. He walks naked to the bathroom.

§

Beneath Albert's open window, Billy and Jamie sit on the wall, in woollen hats, on a silent Laburnum Road. The frosty, unmoving night is textured like layers of coloured cellophane, indigo for the trees, royal blue for the sky, and prickled with stars. Haloed in amber streetlight, they share a joint. Jamie exhales a plume of white smoke into the chill air and recurrently looks up at the window of the upstairs flat. 'Have you taken that book back yet?' he asks.

'Not yet,' Billy says. He shivers and vigorously rubs his arms under a padded jacket.

Jamie kisses Billy. They smile, gently caressing and ruffling each other's hair. 'Goodnight, sleepyhead,' Jamie whispers, as he steps from beneath the amber halo.

'Why don't you stay?' Billy asks. 'We've not seen much of each other.'

'Early start, Billy. And I've no clean clothes with me.'

'I miss you,' Billy says. It's true. Jamie is always so busy with work and perhaps Billy really hasn't made much effort recently. He can feel his life veering off course. How can he be so confused about what he really wants?

'I'll see you on Wednesday, when I come to stay. Three weeks off work. Sleep tight,' Jamie says, giving Billy a brief, but very sweet backward glance, before disappearing into the darkness.

'I'll call you,' Billy whispers, left alone outside the maisonette. He lies back on the wall finishing his joint, gazing up at moonlight through the trees. For a moment, he thinks, he sees Albert's silhouette in the window above. Billy feels himself blanch. Why has he orchestrated this whole carry-on underneath their noses? Though, he knows they will never connect the dots.

He allows the burning orange tip of the joint to dance playfully between the tips of his fingers as he points at the star-prickled sky, counting each, one by one. Then, losing interest he stubs out the joint and slips off the wall. When he turns, he looks up and this time catches Albert in the window. Billy raises a hand to wave, but Albert ducks back, as if pretending not to have seen him.

§

Three nights later Billy knocks on Albert's door. He knocks several times before there is an answer.

'It's rather late, Billy.' Albert lights up the joint he is holding in his hand and breathes out the velvety smoke, watching it slowly dissipate under the harsh, unshaded hallway bulb.

'I'm sorry. I knew you were still up. I could hear you moving around. I've brought something for you.' Billy indicates the large object under his arm.

Albert looks at him rather dubiously. 'I rather thought you'd forgotten me. I've not seen you for days. Better fish to fry. I suppose you've been spending time with that mate of yours. What's his name?'

'Jamie.'

'Oh yes, that's it. I never did get to meet him.'

'Is it okay to come in for a minute? This is pretty heavy.'

Albert pauses for a second. 'It'll have to be Lapsang souchong,' he says. 'I'm clean out of Earl Grey.' He turns and disappears into the kitchen while Billy sidesteps in with the gift he's carried up for Albert, the large canvas he's been working on. He's had it covered up, but now Jamie is actually coming to stay with him, and it's finished, he wants it out of the way. He sets it beside the portrait of Albert that hangs on the wall behind the leather Chesterfield.

Albert returns, skittishly, through the beaded curtain with a tray of cups and saucers and a teapot, hands shaking, spliff in mouth, head tilted back, eyes half closed avoiding smoke. He stoops, places the tray on the coffee table and as he stands up straight again, he speaks around the spliff. 'Ah, Darling boy. What *do* we have here?' Stepping backward to take in the whole piece, he takes a long drag on the joint and passes it to Billy. He stares at the new painting for a few moments before registering the image. Eyes the deepest, bluest, fairy tale blue you ever saw. 'Lord above!' he says, eventually, coughing out smoke at the same time. He clamps his hand over his mouth. 'How did you do this?' His voice breaks. 'How did you do this? Without a model?'

'From your description, from my imagination, from visual references. I don't know. I don't always use a model.

I kind of pick up on a feeling and paint what comes to me.'

'But it's *him*,' Albert says. 'It's extraordinary.' His eyes are full of tears.

'Really?' Billy asks.

'It is uncanny. It's *him*. Alexander Kendall.'

'Alexander Kendall?' Billy asks and he sees at once a look of realisation emerge on Albert's face.

'Yes,' Albert says. 'What are you so—'

'You said, *Alexander Kendall*. You mean *the* Alexander Kendall? From those old films?' Billy is dumbfounded. He thinks of all those movies he's seen at art house cinemas. *I'm Watching You, Behind the Closet, In the Lavender...*

'I didn't tell you?' Albert asks.

'No.' Billy shakes his head in disbelief. 'It really does look like him.'

'Well, I always said you should trust in your own process.'

'He was your...?'

'We were lovers... yes,' Albert says, tears running down his face. 'What have you done, Billy? It's almost as if he's *here* in the room.'

For the first time Billy is stuck for words. 'I... I wanted to give you something,' he says, with reticence. 'You helped me find something. You helped me find my creativity. I wanted to give something back to you.'

'You certainly have, darling, Darling Boy. You've brought him home. Back where he belongs.' Albert blinks away tears.

'This flat? He left it to you?'

'Thank God! I'd have been on the streets otherwise. Caused a terrible fuss with his family. Of-course, they didn't want me to have it. It was more complicated in those days.' Albert smiles, squeezing moisture from his eyes. 'Look at me. Old queen.' He pulls out a handkerchief and wipes his face. 'So, you're painting again?'

'More than ever.' Billy looks away.

'Good!' Albert says, still transfixed by the portrait. 'Drink your tea.' Billy sidles up to him and touches him on the arm, rests his head on his shoulder. 'My God. Look at the eyes, Darling Boy. His eyes are...the colour of...'

'Lapis Lazuli.' Billy smiles, pleased that he can bring the old man a little happiness. 'Mind if I use your loo?'

'You know where it is, Darling Boy.'

Billy's just sat down on the cold black porcelain toilet seat when he hears a knock on Albert's front door—unusual and alarming at this time of night. He listens intently to Albert shuffling to the door and then the sound of the door opening. 'Oh, hello. How may I help you?'

'Er... Hi. I'm looking for Billy. I don't suppose he's here, is he?' There is a silence spiked with tension. 'Sorry, I've just arrived downstairs. He's left all the lights on and this was on the sofa. He was meaning to bring it up, so I thought...' Billy recognises Jamie's voice and he can guess what he has in his hand. *That bloody book!*

'Oh, I've been looking all over for that. I'd forgotten that Billy had it.'

'I've been calling but he's not answering his mobile. I wonder where he's got to... ?'

Billy can hear Albert stuttering in the hallway. 'He... He's on the khazi. He'll be out in a minute. Come in for a drink. I'm sure I have something that will tempt you. I might even have some brandy somewhere.'

Go away, Billy thinks. Then, 'Oh, I never say no to a cup of tea.'

'A man after my own heart,' Albert says.

Billy listens as Jamie steps in and the door slams. There are muffled voices, Albert asking questions that Billy doesn't quite catch. He feels a veil of blackness falling over him and a dragging feeling in his gut as he flushes the loo, washes his hands and steps out of the toilet, into the living room. The muffled conversation suddenly becomes dangerously clear.

'Don't worry,' Albert is saying to Jamie. 'It was going to come out in the end. I'm just shocked he didn't mention it earlier.' Albert and Jamie are standing face to face with the new painting in between the two of them. When Billy steps forward, their eyes meet. Albert's face is pinched and angry. 'So that's why you've been avoiding me,' he says, glaring at Billy. 'Don't you think it would have been kind to tell me, Darling Boy?'

'I'm sorry,' Billy says, swallowing on guilt. He doesn't know what to say. He shakes his head unable to comprehend the whole perverse situation. What is Jamie doing here in Albert's flat? He can feel an outpouring of honesty coming, but is halted by Albert's next unexpected words:

'Moving into a flat in Dalston and you didn't think to tell me.'

Jamie waves at Billy, smiling, eyes beaming obliviously. 'You left this downstairs.' He's holding Albert's copy of *The Complete Guide to Recreational Psychoactives*. 'I thought I'd bring it up.'

'I thought you weren't coming until tomorrow,' Billy says.

'I wanted to surprise you.'

Billy cringes. He feels his phone vibrating in his pocket with received messages.

Albert points at Jamie, 'If it hadn't been for this young man, I would have known nothing about it.' He stops and looks at Jamie. 'I'm sorry, sir, I didn't catch your name.'

Billy wants to leap across the room and press his hands over Jamie's mouth. For a moment, it is as if time has slowed down and Jamie's mouth opens at the speed of treacle pouring from a tin. And then...

'Jamie,' Jamie says, beaming at Billy.

Albert pauses. He looks shocked. There is a need, just for a moment, for silence. Eventually, Albert looks directly at Billy. In a moment, a knowledge passes between them. Jamie looks at them both, a realisation forming.

'Is it possible, do you think... to be *in love* with more than one person at the same time?' Albert asks.

Billy is stunned into silence for a moment. He cautiously considers his answer. Finally, he quietly replies, 'No.'

Albert closes his eyes, his head taut with sadness. He looks as if he's been winded. 'No, I didn't think so.'

§

87

After all of Billy's *I-didn't-mean-to-hurt-yous*, Jamie goes back downstairs, out of the way. Billy stands next to Albert, who is resting against the window frame. Above the flats, a texture-less bruise of luminous grey-yellow spreads itself across the sky, like a patch of backlit vellum. Albert leans out of his first floor window as the first fork of lightning streaks across Laburnum Road. The cobblestones look like rivets in brown PVC, an effect of amber streetlight in spent rainwater. Billy can smell the sickly sweet stink of mildew, rising from a winter sludge, rotting on the pavement. Albert opens the window wide letting in the cool charged air. A storm is coming, he thinks, anticipating an impending thunderclap. Then it comes, not a clap, but a low hellish rumble, like the amplified sound of an impatient belly. He watches as Albert nods to himself, loosening his tie and the buttons of his shirt and moving silently away from the window.

§

'Please stop,' Billy says, pursuing Jamie around the kitchen as he collects his things to leave. He's forcing clothes and his writing pad back into his holdall. 'Can we at least talk about it?'

'And listen to another pack of lies?' Jamie says, his voice trembling. His widow's peak and receding hairline makes him look rather more serious than he used to. His choice of clothes has taken on a streamlined, utilitarian look that fits in well with those academic types at the art gallery.

Billy feels tears coming. He feels desperate, grasping. 'One minute you're stifling me, needy, the next you're remote, closed off, wrapped up in that bloody job. If you weren't so… maybe I wouldn't feel the need to lie. Maybe I wouldn't—'

'So this is all my fault?' Jamie stops now, drops the holdall and turns on him. 'The drugs, the booze, the endless nocturnal excursions…' His face is contorted with fury. 'I *drove* you to it?'

'I didn't say that.' Billy says. 'But sometimes—'

'How could you? He's old enough to be your grandfather.'

'I just wanted to have some fun.'

Hot tears sting Billy's cheeks. He watches Jamie wrench on his jacket, pick up his bag and walk to the front door.

'Some *fun*? I hope it was worth it.'

§

The next day, Billy knows he has to visit Albert one last time. Static dust particles in the air are visibly disturbed as Billy enters the still and silent passageway up to Albert's flat. Why has he made such a mess of this? All trace of what has been before is now gone. Any semblance of an affair has now been extinguished. A little piece of him has disappeared. Maybe it hasn't been there for a while. No longer can he locate that piece of him that can make everything better, the part that could make Jamie stop crying.

As he reaches the top of the stairs, he stops. The door is ajar. In the rehearsal in his head, he'd been expecting to knock, perhaps repeatedly, and maybe have to force his way in. He knows Albert would turn him away. But he knows he must at least get in to try to make amends. But now he makes a different entrance.

Peering around the open door. Billy's breath quickens, hairs stand out on his skin. His eyes fix on the empty space between the wooden floor and the old man's feet—a ray of sunlight picks out the dust floating there. On the floor—a fallen stepladder. Billy's heart makes one violent thud, as if it has stopped. After that, there's a squeaking noise that sounds like seagulls crying. His heart beats so hard and fast his ears throb. Why can't he scream? He wobbles and loses his footing. His vision pulses dark blue at the periphery, as if the lights are dimming. He gags, and his vomit hits the floor.

Albert, hanging by his neck from a rope: face blue and swollen like a pumpkin, tongue sticking out, eyes bulging. He is wearing a white vest and underpants, yellowed and damp with urine. His hands, too, are swollen and reddened.

Billy regains himself to take in the full picture and tries to control his breathing. He wipes his mouth on his sleeve. He wants to sit but can't, not in the room with… He can't just leave. No. What? What? He averts his eyes from the body, moving further into the room. Sunlight reflects off the Chesterfield where he and Albert had sex. The large portrait of Alexander leans against the wall. Above, is the painting of Albert Power, a young man.

Out of breath, he takes his mobile phone from his pocket. He looks down at the floor, thinking about Jamie on his way to work. Who to call? The police? An ambulance? No, that would be pointless; Albert is dead.

Billy walks to the open window, rainwater on the sill, and looks out. He takes a deep breath. Everything on Laburnum Road is quiet and peaceful. No-one around. A crisp December day. He turns and stands in the bay window where Albert has arranged a bunch of freshly cut flowers in a green glass vase. Bright pink gerberas on long elegant stems, just like the ones he'd first seen Albert buying in the market. Then he sees the bureau, open, where Billy had previously pilfered a couple of wraps of cocaine. Pulling open little wooden drawers inside, he discovers pills and powders and vials of liquid lying inside. He recognises—coke, crack, heroin, K, ecstasy, LSD, GHB—the whole chemistry set. Fuck. Albert had a whole cottage industry up here. His shaking fingers move across the folding desk shelf of the bureau. There is also a little plastic bag with what look like droplets of glass inside. Crystal Meth. He fingers the contents of the bag between his thumb and index finger. He looks down at the pills. He's never seen so many drugs. He finds his hands are on them and he's stuffing his pockets with packets and bottles. And then he sees the letter. It's addressed to Billy Monroe. He picks it up and reads:

My dearest, Darling Boy,

I'm such an old fool. I don't know what I'm doing here. I don't belong anymore. I'm sad and I'm lonely. I've had this infantile idea that we could have been in love. Now I'm embarrassed by my own foolishness. Finally, after all these years, I thought I'd found someone I could be close to, someone who could make smaller the void of Alexander's death. It's ridiculous, isn't it, to think that someone like you could love someone like me?

You came into my life like a flash of lightning—a boy running in summertime. Seeing you was like seeing him come back to my life. It was unreal. In you, I felt him. But the kind of love he once had for me, I know you seem to have now found in another. I'm crushed by the idea that you cannot be mine entirely. But I'm just a creepy old man. It would be wrong to take this time from someone more able to enjoy your vitality.

I can't lift myself out of this darkness which I suspect, if I'm honest, is chemical—a result of the years I have used substances. And in any case, I'm a dead man walking. The ravens are circling. I can't remember how I got into all this—this vampirous existence. I pray you will not let this happen to you. I pray that you will live a long and happy life with the person who you choose to share your life.

I have a deep affection for you but I am terrified of looking into your eyes, to find the feeling unrequited. And were the feeling reciprocated, it would be scandalous. It only serves to remind me of that other devotion I still harbour for Alexander.

Without him, the winter days are long. Shadows surround me in this lonely flat. I can feel my soul creeping from my body, this empty husk, to find the place where he now dwells. We are shackled, you and I, in this most inappropriate and addictive relationship. Who would accept love between someone like you and someone like me? Meeting you was a joy but, nonetheless a heartache. I can't go on. I'm not the same man anymore.

You have helped me reach this place. You have helped me to realise who I am. So it is time for me to break our shackles. They say that people who write letters like this don't actually mean to do it. But I do. I have the rope that will pull me into the next world, to help me make my leap into the unknown. My only hope is that he will be there, waiting for me.

Maybe some day, we shall meet again, in another condition, my darling, Darling Boy.

All my love

Albert

Acknowledgements

The Pharmacist has had a number of incarnations, firstly as my debut release with the wonderful Salt Publishing and then as an episode within my larger collection of 'working-class' stories, *He's Done Ever So Well for Himself*.

This particular paperback edition has been a long time in the making and, as such, there have been a lot of people who have supported and inspired me along the way. There have been the crazy chaotic boyfriends and the sensible organised ones, there have been the four-in-the-morning friends, the friends who paid for dinner when I have been skint, the writing group friends who gave feedback on very raw drafts; there were the friends who made me start, the friends who told me not to give up and the friends who insisted I finish. There are that merry gang of lovely, supportive friends who turn up to readings and buy books and cheer and bouy me through the writer's life. And, of course, there has been Albert and Billy and Jamie and Gloria who have haunted my days and my nights, and who still do.

For their continued support throughout this whole process, my undying gratitude goes to the to the following: my beautiful boyfriend—Nathan Evans, my parents – Joy and Dave Ward, Kit de Waal, David Cabreza, Elizabeth Pisani, Michael Jones, Gustav Grass, David Cabaret, Andrew Wilkinson, Alex Hopkins, João Florêncio, Jonathan Kemp, Rebecca Carter, Jason Ford, Alice Adams, Anne Tillyer, Petronella Carter, Amy Redmond, Tessa Garland, Marcel Baettig, Anna Sutton, Bea Symes, James Maker, Paul Buchanan, Lisa Goldman, Sophie Morgan, Joshua Davies, Bartholomew Bennett, Annie Murray, Gaylene Gould, Jake Jones, Kat Dixon, Matthew Westwood, Michael Barry, Michael Bradley, Karen Livingstone, Polly Wiseman, Anthony Psaila, Emma Bourgeois, Toby Rye, Katie Vermont, Simon Reeves, Bryanne McIntosh-Melville, Eddie Doherty, Chris Atherton, Neil McKenna and Daren Kay. To Andrew M Pisanu for his beautiful music. To the divine Scott Humpheys for being Billy on the cover and to my bestie, Joe Mateo, for stepping up as an amazing cover designer.

Thank you to Christopher and Jen Hamilton-Emery, who helped early on in this journey and who continue to do so.

Special thanks to Uli Lenart and Jimmy MacSweeney at the very splendid Gay's the Word Bookshop.

Also from Inkandescent

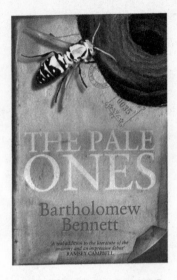

THE PALE ONES
by Bartholomew Bennett

Few books ever become loved. Most linger on undead, their sallow pages labyrinths of old, brittle stories and screeds of forgotten knowledge... And other things, besides: Paper-pale forms that rustle softly through their leaves. Ink-dark shapes swarming in shadow beneath faded type. And an invitation...

Harris delights in collecting the unloved. He wonders if you'd care to donate. A small something for the odd, pale children no-one has seen. An old book, perchance? Neat is sweet; battered is better. Broken spine or torn binding, stained or scarred - ugly doesn't matter. Not a jot. And if you've left a little of yourself between the pages – a receipt or ticket, a mislaid letter, a scrawled note or number – that's just perfect. He might call on you again.

Hangover Square meets Naked Lunch through the lens of a classic M. R. James ghost story. To hell and back again (and again) through Whitby, Scarborough and the Yorkshire Moors. Enjoy your Mobius-trip.

'A real addition to the literature of the uncanny and an impressive debut for its uncompromising author.'
RAMSEY CAMPBELL

Also from Inkandescent

He's Done Ever So Well For Himself
by Justin David

As a little boy, growing up in the half of the country decimated by the harsh economics of Mrs Thatcher, Jamie dreams of rubbing shoulders with the glamorous creatures from the pages of *Smash Hits* – only to discover years later that once amongst them, the real stars in his life are the ones he left behind.

Not least, his mother Gloria whose one-liners and put-downs are at as colourful as her pink furry mules and DayGlo orange dungarees. All of this, she carries off with the panache of a television landlady.

Jamie swaps the high heels and high hair of 80s Midlands for the high expectations of London at the heart of 90s Cool Britannia. He's drawn towards a new family of misfits, fuelled by drugs and sexual experimentation – from which he must ultimately untangle himself in order to fulfil his dreams. This bitingly funny tale of conflict and self-discovery is *page-turning friction.*

'*For anyone who's lived and loved and fought to be the person they're meant to be*'
MATT CAIN

Also from Inkandescent

AutoFellatio
by James Maker

According to Wikipedia, only a few men can actually perform the act of auto-fellatio. We never discover whether James Maker—from rock bands Raymonde and RPLA—is one of them. But certainly, as a story-teller and raconteur, he is one in a million.

From Bermondsey enfant terrible to Valencian grande dame—a journey that variously stops off at Morrissey Confidant, Glam Rock Star, Dominatrix, Actor and Restoration Man—his long and winding tale is a compendium of memorable bons mots woven into a patchwork quilt of heart-warming anecdotes that make you feel like you've hit the wedding-reception jackpot by being unexpectedly seated next the groom's witty homosexual uncle.

More about the music industry than about coming out, this remix is a refreshing reminder that much of what we now think of as post-punk British rock and pop, owes much to the generation of musicians like James. The only criticism here is that – as in life – fellatio ultimately cums to an end.

'a glam-rock Naked Civil Servant in court shoes. But funnier. And tougher'
MARK SIMPSON

Also from Inkandescent

THREADS
by Nathan Evans & Justin David

If Alice landed in London not Wonderland this book might be the result.
Threads is the first collection from Nathan Evans, each poem complemented
by a bespoke photograph from Justin David and, like Tenniel's illustrations
for Carroll, picture and word weft and warp to create an alchemic (rabbit)
whole.

On one page, the image of an alien costume, hanging surreally beside
a school uniform on a washing line, accompanies a poem about fleeing
suburbia. On another, a poem about seeking asylum accompanies the
image of another displaced alien on an urban train. Spun from heartfelt
emotion and embroidered with humour, Threads will leave you aching with
longing and laughter.

> 'In this bright and beautiful collaboration, poetry and photography
> join hands, creating sharp new ways to picture our lives and loves.'
> NEIL BARTLETT

> 'Two boldly transgressive poetic voices'
> MARISA CARNESKY

Also from Inkandescent

SWANSONG
by Nathan Evans

A gentleman called Joan lands in a subdued, suburban care home like a colourful, combustible cocktail. A veteran of Gay Lib, he dons battle dress and seeks an ally in the young, gay but disappointingly conventional care assistant Craig for his assault on the heteronormativity of the care system. Then, in this most unlikely of settings, Joan is offered love by a gentleman called Jim...

This bittersweet comedy explores issues surrounding care and LGBT elders. It premiered at the Royal Vauxhall Tavern, London on 17 October 2018, presented by 89th Productions as part of And What? Queer Arts Festival.

'Side-splittingly funny and achingly romantic.
A play about ageing disgracefully that's ferociously full of life.'
RIKKI BEADLE-BLAIR

Also from Inkandescent

FEMME FATALE
by Polly Wiseman

1968, New York. Nico, The Velvet Underground's glamorous front woman, is waiting to shoot Andy Warhol's latest movie when her room is invaded by Valerie Solanas, writer of the radical SCUM Manifesto. A battle to the death begins. Can these two iron-willed opponents become allies and change their futures?

With women's ownership of their stories and bodies still firmly on the news agenda, Femme Fatale draws parallels between 1960s feminism and today. It was first presented in Sussex and London in September and October 2019.

'Wiseman's writing sears and burns'
THE GUARDIAN

Also from Inkandescent

CNUT

by Nathan Evans

'Poignant, humane and uncompromising'
STEPHEN MORRISON-BURKE

As King Cnut proved, tide and time wait for no man:
An AnthropoScene, the first part of this collection, dives into the rising tides of geo-political change, the second, Our Future Is Now Downloading, explores sea-changes of more personal natures.

Nathan's debut, Threads, was longlisted for the Polari First Book Prize. His follow-up bears all the watermarks of someone who's swum life's emotional spectrum. Short and (bitter)sweet, this is poetry for a mobile generation, poetry for sharing – often humorous, always honest about contemporary human experience, saying more in a few lines than politicians say in volumes, it offers an antidote to modern living.

'a kaleidoscopic journey brimming with vivid imagery, playfulness and warmth—a truly powerful work'
KEITH JARRETT

Inkandescent Publishing was created in 2016
by Justin David and Nathan Evans to shine a light on
diverse and distinctive voices.

Sign up to our mailing list to stay informed
about future releases:

www.inkandescent.co.uk

by outsiders for outsiders

follow us on Facebook:

@InkandescentPublishing

and on Twitter:

@InkandescentUK